ENNEMONDE

Angelo
The Battle of Pavia (1525)
To the Slaughterhouse
Two Riders of the Storm

JEAN GIONO

Ennemonde

A NOVEL
TRANSLATED FROM THE FRENCH
BY DAVID LE VAY

PETER OWEN · LONDON

ISBN 0 7206 2801 6

Translated from the French
Ennemonde et autres caractères

PETER OWEN LIMITED
12 Kendrick Mews Kendrick Place London SW7

First British Commonwealth edition 1970
© Editions Gallimard 1968
English translation © Peter Owen 1970

Printed in Great Britain by
Bristol Typesetting Co Ltd
Barton Manor St Philips Bristol

I

Wisely, the roads circumvent the High Country. Some farms are ten or twenty kilometres from their nearest neighbour; often a solitary man would have to cover those kilometres to encounter another solitary man, but he never does so in his whole life; or maybe a tribe of adults, children and old folk might approach another tribe of adults, children and old folk—but to see what? Women broken down by repeated pregnancies, ruddy men and rotten-ripe old people (the children too), and all only to be looked down on? To hell with it! If one wants to show oneself off, there are the village fairs. Thirty or forty kilometres separate the villages, which are sited carefully at the periphery where the road goes.

On the land: beeches, chestnuts, oaks, beeches more and more gigantic and tall as one penetrates deeper, more and more millenary; far from all truck with men, families of birches, very beautiful in summer, that disappear, white on white, in the snow; on the moors: lavender, broom, alfalfa, sedges, dandelions, then stones, stones rounded as if rivers had once flowed at these heights, farthest of all flat stones as sonorous as bells, echoing the least sound—the leap of a cricket, the footfall of a mouse, the slither of a viper, or the wind that takes hold of these telluric springboards.

The sky is often black, or rather a deep marine blue, but one's impression of it is the same as one receives from black; except at that season when a wild mignonette flowers whose delicate odour is so joyful as to dissipate all melancholy. Apart from this season of the mignonette the fine weather here is not gay; it's not sad either, it's something else, those whom it suits can't do without it. The bad weather is very attractive, it assumes all at once a cosmic appeal. There is something galactic or even extra-galactic about its behaviour. It doesn't rain here like anywhere else, it feels as if God is dealing with it personally; the wind here takes the fate of the world firmly in hand. Storms here have special manifestations; there is no lightning and no sound but every metal object simply begins to glow—belt-buckles, shoe-studs, fasteners, spectacles, bracelets, rings, chains, etc., one must touch oneself with caution. Twenty or thirty superb beeches can often be seen side by side, carbonized, upright, blackened, dead from head to foot, witness that something has happened in this silence.

The twilight is oftener green rather than red and it lasts a very long time, so long that in the end one is forced to see that night has fallen and that the glow now comes from the stars. They give a good light here, often enough to recognize someone on the road. Perhaps there are more to be seen here than elsewhere; at any rate, what's certain is that they're bigger due to the air here— either because its purity, which is extreme, shows off the constellations vividly, or because it contains a substance acting as a lens. No one here boasts of having been abroad on a dark night; should it be foreseeable, one clears off

6

before it arrives. There is a code of conduct laid down by our ancestors concerning this country that gives excellent results, a single rule : to conform to it. All the accidents that have been known to happen—and they are innumerable, some of them peculiar—result from breaking this kind of rule or law.

Nothing is easier, for instance, than to go from Villesèche to the Pas de Redortier in broad daylight, it takes only an hour. The landscape is not very encouraging but it's feasible and takes only a little willpower (if it's for hunting) or stupidity (if it's gratuitous). But on a day when the clouds are low and heavy and it gets dark, go ahead, no one will chance it !

The tool the people here have most often to hand is the rifle, whether it's a matter of hunting or, shall we say, philosophical reflection; in the one case as in the other there is no solution without a shot. The rifle hangs from a glass stem fixed to the wall by the *patron*'s chair; whether the latter is at table or by the fire, the rifle is always within reach. It's not that the country lacks security from the point of view of law and order; on the contrary, even in the heyday of brigandage, there was never any crime up here—except for one in 1928, and that was precisely a matter of what is to be feared here, which is solitude. Family life is no remedy for this, at best these are gatherings of recluses who, in reality, each go their own way; the families are not centred round anyone, they move outwards from someone. And then, sure enough, there is metaphysics, not that of the Sorbonne, but that which one is forced to take into account by reason of the hostility of the irremediable

7

silence and of the world. M. Sartre wouldn't be much use here, whereas a rifle can be useful over and over again.

It may seem astonishing that these peasants haven't the plough-handle oftener in their grasp; it's because these peasants are shepherds. It's this, too, that keeps them remote from (and above) mechanical progress. No one has yet invented a machine to watch sheep. It is the father, the *patron*, who runs the flock, the son or sons who manage the small-scale agricultural set-up that is, in any case, a closed economy. Only the ground needed for the wheat, barley, potatoes and vegetables essential to individual or family life is cultivated, and that is why so many of these peasants stay unmarried and live alone; they need so little then that they scratch the ground for barely more than one month in the year.

For the use of the most vigorous bachelors there still existed, not thirty years ago, a Mohammedan paradise. This was a house in a shaded spot, the most sinister imaginable, which never saw the sun even at the height of summer. A widow lived there; she was a good sixty years old at that time. When a bachelor paid her a visit she put out a flag over her door, a flag such as you or I might use, a tricolour, blue, white and red, the most official of flags. And, in fact, it came from the town-hall of Saint-C., where it had been allocated for the celebration of the 14th of July. The visit over, the widow took the flag in again. It was well known. There was never any fuss about it. Until the day when someone attempted to modernize these arrangements. A young woman from Avignon, doubtless accomplished at the game and smart

8

into the bargain, thought she could increase the takings by delivering the merchandise to the home. For one summer she was famous, then she disappeared without trace. It was rumoured immediately that she had been seen at the fair at Laragne. But Laragne is a long way off. She had a gentleman-friend who came to make enquiries all around. He was not likeable, so they led him up the garden-path. He tried to make a fuss but it was no use. He must have suffered a blow to his pride, for he went off—and this is not done—to tell his story at the *gendarmerie* at Sault. In the course of the enquiry the presence of the young woman at the fair at Laragne, and even the one at Gap, was confirmed by over fifty witnesses who were evidently of good faith and, no less evidently, not up to much. It was not till some three or four years later that someone found some odds and ends, long rummaged over by the foxes. But in these high-lands odds and ends are not hard to come by. The widow did not shut up shop till she was over eighty. But, as it happened, she'd saved nothing but the flag, which she'd kept and which was, I believe, placed on her bier at the funeral and planted on her tomb, where the wind and rain finally tore it to shreds; but I saw it.

The women here are shapeless bundles of second-rate materials. It's not from any lack of desire to show off, on the contrary they rather strive to outdo each other, but the merchants at the fairs prefer to cater for peasant snobbishness rather than sell good merchandise. The women don't go in for spotted materials any more, or for the jet that suited their grandmothers so well, they want the latest fashion. It's chucked at them. This suits them as an apron does a pig and the colours would make an architect cry out (which isn't saying much) but one has to show that one's got money. So much so that if a woman is seen to be tastefully dressed, a princess among all these lumps, it's a safe bet that she is poor and ashamed of herself. Sometimes the very old women make a great impression. Past the age of pregnancy they discover a second body; even those who remain bulky reshape themselves, but the thin assume a true nobility. This is also the period when those who've no more money go back to the old cretonnes; for in every family there's something decent (which everyone detests).

The young girls, as long as they're virgins, have the bloom of fruit, then this beauty shatters and the splinters of it are to be seen in the children. They retain absolutely nothing of their former state; some Venuses become frightful monsters, they nearly all have the mouths of the seventeenth century, toothless or, even worse, with a few great loose teeth that they suck. That's abominable enough. But one mustn't take their gangling appearance at its face value. They are almost always domineering women. They do marvels when they're up against it. One thinks, still, of Ennemonde Girard.

She was born Martin and spent the bloom of her youth at Le Gaur des Oulles, in the narrow valley that separates le Ventoux from Lure. She intended to become a teacher but failed her entrance examination to the teachers' training college. Back on her farm, she looked after the sheep. On the shaded slopes of the mountains, over towards the col de la Croix-de-l'Homme mort, she got into the habit, once a week, of meeting a young man from Séderon who brought loads of wood over the mountains destined for the jam factories at Apt and the bakeries of the Calavon valley. This was at the end of the '14 war; at that time the furnaces were still fuelled with faggots of white oak. This lad, Honoré Girard, though he claimed to be from Séderon, where indeed his parents were settled, came from Chamoune and even from Reychasset. That is to say, from what is known here as the 'tiger country'. It is a labyrinth of gloomy valleys where, long ago, the more intransigent heretics took refuge. Until around 1950 the pastors who directed the souls of these people (and very narrow they were) protested violently even against Protestantism and imposed some very acrobatic spiritual gymnastics on their flock. These trapeze artistes were generally distrusted. But how to find fault with blue eyes, a fine aquiline nose, well-made features, a supple body and a vocabulary enriched by the Old Testament, when one has failed the entrance examination to the teachers' training college? Every Friday around three o'clock Ennemonde drove her flock towards the road where Honoré Girard had halted his carts.

Despite the thick woods and the pretty enclosures of broom Ennemonde got married in white. The young couple took as a farm a shepherd's hut on the height of the hill of le Pendu, ten kilometres from Ferrassière. It was a good spot, capable of supporting two hundred sheep. They started with twenty ewes, cleared their six hectares, and were solidly established by their second year.

From the start Honoré insisted on his wife's wearing

a nightdress with a hole in it. This is a long armour of heavy material that permits the making of children without sinful embellishment. It was by this somewhat irksome procedure that she had five children in four and a half years, then one every year up to thirteen. First she lost about twenty teeth and then got rid of the remaining ones with the point of a knife. She was obese, with enormous buttocks; it seems her husband's belt would not go round the base of her thigh; on the other hand her chest became flat, but she kept her beautiful glossy black hair (she wasn't forty yet) and, marvel of marvels, extraordinarily slender ankles.

They may have had no money but they had bought the house (from a count at Carpentras) and rented pasture, and Honoré's flock of nearly three hundred animals was famous. The buyers always saw him before anyone else. Life was good, despite the nightshirt with a hole in it, about which he was not open to compromise. He was fond enough of good living and the winter was passed stacking small plates on big ones. He had no idea about wine but that's an ignorance common to the region; he refreshed himself like everyone else with some vinegar from Gignac. Ennemonde, for want of anything better, was an excellent cook, she devoted herself to it; everything was used—thrushes, plover, young wild boar, hares. They killed two pigs a year, one in the autumn, the other in spring; and someone with foresight might have predicted certain future events on seeing how much Ennemonde enjoyed grinding by hand the mixture of minced liver and fat in the family pork-butchery.

Honoré claimed that all this was in the Bible. But something happened to him that was not in the Bible. Honoré began to 'shrink'. That's a term that's used here for a common enough phenomenon. When a man (or a woman) no longer has enough curiosity about the natural world he takes refuge in the unnatural. Unnatural but sometimes very commonplace—not to undress any more, for instance, or to stop talking or walking, no longer to visit a certain town or a certain fair, not to see anyone again; often it's as stupid as no longer putting one's hands in one's pockets, never cleaning one's spectacles or removing one's hat. I suppose this is done in the hope that the world minus something, no matter what, will be different from the everyday world. And in fact it must work since those who shrink in this way never regain their normal stature. The unnatural is not always limited to the banal, however, and some have shrunk to such an extent as to have succeeded in insinuating themselves into an extraordinary world. Thus, Numa Pallisson, for instance, lived for two years on good terms with a community of crows at the top of a beech twenty metres high. He bolted the eggs from the nests and, for drink in the summer, drew blood from a bird. He died up there and the winged creatures ended by eating him. But to return to Honoré.

He did not make his retreat on a very lordly scale, but it was a nuisance all the same; he decided not to sell anything any more, neither ewes nor lambs nor sheep. The flock multiplied unrestrainedly but the area of pasture remained the same. The lambs developed rickets, the ewes died. The survivors were all skin and bone. The buyers, abused at first at each appearance, no longer came near the accursed flock. Ennemonde, deprived of bare necessities, began to find it too much to stomach. She immediately took action. She ensured the complicity of her first six children, the oldest. This was easy and with their complicity she possessed herself of the rifle. Honoré was relegated forthwith to second, and indeed to fifth, place, the fifth wheel of the cart. Ennemonde was sensible enough to leave him the where-withal to satisfy his obsession—twenty animals that she undertook not to touch, but not twenty-one, twenty—so long as she had the sale of the lambs. She dealt with the rest in masterly fashion, gun in sling, with her two oldest who were at that time fifteen and fourteen respect-ively. That is to say, men. She was quickly and unani-mously accepted as the *patronne*. It is now that her story intersects with that of Clef-des-coeurs, but we shall see more of that when we come to speak of that person-age.

What followed is normal and uneventful. Honoré was killed a few years later by a kick from a mule, at least so it was supposed and it may very well be true. He did own one that was very stubborn. His corpse was found between the nag's hoofs in the stable, his head smashed in, and the mark of the shoes was quite apparent. What more can one want?

The males of these parts don't make grand old men. They make old bones; it isn't rare to come across some over ninety years old and quite a few near the century, but they become overripe after eighty. Those who kept in good trim until then, and even seemed set to improve further, collapse, crumple up, and become prey to the worms before death, which is then only a formality demanded by the law. One could bury them in good faith without this formality. Unfortunately, this is forbidden. They make old bones, they do not make old souls. This is due to the fact that they lose their hearts early on; some no longer have any by the age of ten, others have none even at birth, the best rid themselves of this useless muscle quite naturally around twenty-five. People who are mere passers-by, or those who are only superficially acquainted with the country, do not notice this; the old folk remain deceptive in most cases until the day when it becomes clear that, in these cases, the heart was unnecessary. The day when it is necessary one is confronted with monoliths.

Certainly, these are civilized people. They are much more civilized even than other peasants or other recluses and, in particular, they have an understanding of things a great deal more acute than that of the inhabitants of the Low Country. With strangers—and they regard as strangers anyone who has not lived in the heights for centuries—they are polite, courteous, affable, kind, agreeable, obliging. It's just that they have no real relations with strangers. They tolerate certain things of a stranger, even if it entails firing a warning shot rather brutally should the need arise. With their equals they give no warning, they act at once, without delay and without pity.

This realistic mode of behaviour may seem at first to accord ill with the fact that they inhabit a region where life exists only by means of a constant injection of unreality (as we shall see). But, in fact, reality pushed to the extreme connects precisely with unreality. To go to the heart of things is to accept their myth, certainly not to deny it.

The life they lead here does not encourage generosity. The Dianes de Montemayor, the Pastors Fido, the Astrées and the Marie-Antoinettes spread the idea of the sheepfolds as peaceful homesteads. Who more agreeable than men who live constantly with the animal adopted by the wisdom of nations as the paragon of gentleness: gentle as a lamb? But the lamb is not gentle, it is stupid. The ram is an aggressive animal, the ewe is a direct descendant of the bestiality trials of the Middle Ages. It is in the company of this stupidity, this aggressiveness and this unhealthy temptation that the men of these parts live all the days that God makes, and in the most utter solitude.

For the common run of mortals the shepherd is a man who dreams, leaning on his crook. He dreams right enough. What else could you expect him to do? But he is in the position of being tempted, at every moment, to realize his dreams, without very much hindrance. He has only to discard certain laws, certain precepts, certain customs. It's soon done. What more appetizing than to evade the law and deride custom? Especially when the life one leads is hard—wind, cold, snow, rain, fear; not the fear we all know, which grips us and from which we emerge, but that endemic fear from which one does not emerge!

God preserve us from the shepherd's dream! Genghis Khan was a shepherd. The sheep's eye is an aperture through which one may surreptitiously regard the voluptuous revels of animality. Plainly, one would not, after that, go and raze Samarkand or build pyramids of thousands of severed heads on the banks of the Oxus —but that's because one is single-handed; the desire is not lacking, it's a question of numbers. So then one thinks of what one can do in one's small domain; there are the fairs, the feast-days, the families. Sometimes one succeeds in doing fine enough things, sometimes not; the circumstances are not always propitious. One is sometimes involved with characters who resist, families that won't let themselves be wiped out, children who grow quickly, adversaries who have also gazed into the sheep's eye. Since what matters is not so much to win as to have available at all times the wherewithal to continue the game, family and society remain apparently intact.

One day, at the col du Négron, a bloodstained velvet coat is found. Not merely bloodstained, and vilely, that is with shreds of flesh, but torn and chewed as if by a tiger. Enquiry is made on all sides but no one recognizes the coat. Enquiry is made everywhere if someone has disappeared: No. So it's a stranger's coat. He can fuck himself! People stop bothering about it. The *gendarmes* pay three more little visits, then go away.

It was in April. The service-berries flowered in the valleys; on the heights the fox-tails began to redden. The shaded glens oozed with streamlets. This is the time of rumours in the High Country. The very grass seems to re-echo. When the wind stops blowing it's not silence that follows but a thousand stifled noises. There are no bird songs; the thrushes, quail, plover, robins, tits, etc., stay down below, in the valleys, only the monotonous cry of the eagle is heard for a short space around four o'clock in the evenings. The crows and rooks are in their nests.

That same year, at the Richards (of Saumane), the flock had been divided in two and one part of the flock had been entrusted to the oldest, Siméon. This was a lad of fourteen; but he had already gazed into the sheep's eye. One afternoon, in his pasture and at least fifteen kilometres from le Négron, he was at the summit, and overlooking the long shaded slopes that descend almost vertically towards the Jabron, when he heard a bizarre outcry in the thickets of white oak and holly that clothe the hillside. This outcry was accompanied by rustlings of dry leaves, as if from the passage of some large animal. There are often boars in these parts. He took hold of his shot-gun and waited.

Nothing arrived except nightfall. Siméon returned to his hut, which was about a kilometre away, brought in his sheep and barricaded himself in. The Richards' farm is twenty kilometres away but Siméon had owned an ejector shot-gun for some months and he ran no risk of letting himself be impressed by any unorthodox happenings. He loaded his double barrels with big game cartridges and lay down near the door.

He was woken in the middle of the night by a strong smell (it stank like the devil!) and also by his dog, which came trembling to shelter against him. The smell was frightful. Siméon also heard an animal snuffling under the door, then it scratched. He dared not move or open up; he had to stay still. That is what the little shepherd did.

He wasn't so very brave in the morning! But the flock had to be put out. A trace of the abominable odour still lingered. However, if one can't trust an ejector shot-gun, what can one trust? Let's jolly well get on with it; he opened the door. He saw clearly that something had moved across the small yard where the water-troughs and salt-trays were situated and the sheep themselves were aware of it, for they refused their salt at this spot; but there are no giants in the morning, or lions, everything is of normal size and what is of normal size can normally be dealt with by an ejector shot-gun, especially one that is perfectly choked on the left and perfectly half-choked on the right, and with barrels of Hercules steel.

He killed the horrible thing a little before noon. The sun was already heavy, the flock, replete, moved at a snail's pace under the heat. But once he had left the hut the hound pricked up his ears and did not lose sight of his master who, shot-gun in hand, did not lose sight of his hound. They were both on the alert. Suddenly the dog made a very quiet sound, just enough to alert his master without disturbing the sheep, whom it did not concern, and Siméon saw emerging from behind a heap of stones a small animal at which he fired his two barrels without more ado, saying to himself: 'That looks like two dogs tied together, but what is it they're dragging between them?' It was, in fact, two dogs attached to a corpse that they had been dragging about for two days.

Siméon returned his flock to the fold and went running off to warn his fellows, who were grazing their sheep some kilometres lower down. The *gendarmes* climbed up. The explanation was forthcoming or, more exactly, an explanation.

The search might have lasted a hundred and seven years. Who would have thought of establishing a link between the bloody coat of le Négron and Jules Dupuis, called Bouscarle? The Dupuis are far from strangers, there are Dupuis daughters in nine families out of ten; there are the Dupuis called Renifle, the Dupuis called Sans-travail, the Dupuis called Melchior, the Dupuis called Automobile, the Dupuis Tête-de-fer, the Dupuis-Charbotte and this Dupuis, called Bouscarle (i.e. wagtail), whose disappearance no one could be aware of since he lived alone like a leper on a mountain slope as dark as a cauldron over towards Pompe, where no one ever goes. Go and see if he's there or if he's not there; and if he's not there go and see if he has disappeared or if he's gone to fetch provisions from Omergues or Séderon, Montfroc or even as far as Châteauneuf-Miravail.

The fact is that he never moved around without two dogs fastened to his belt. This habit arose from a punch-up he'd had with a certain Martin, from Montbrun. And this almost brings us back to Ennemonde Girard, for this famous Martin was her first cousin and even, to some extent, her boy-friend when she was still trying for the teachers' training college. Later on, we shall see this Martin come a cropper; but, not long after the cousins, male and female, had done with Ennemonde, he had difficulties with the police. Note that I say police, and not *gendarmes*. Here, generally, the *gendarmes* suffice; whereas, for this specimen, persons came from afar off, from Digne and even, I believe, from Marseilles. I don't precisely know what it was all about at that time, there was talk of a search, people hinted at the theft of postal packages; for my part I'm not very sure and anyway they let him go.

He ran a service with a broken-down coach between Montbrun and Sisteron and it was as the result of a discussion in this coach that he fought with Dupuis, called Bouscarle. This happened at the col de Macuègne, above Barret. The two men, who were alone in the vehicle, climbed down on to the road and beat each other up. Bouscarle had the best of it and Martin declared that he would 'have his skin' at the first opportunity. Hence the two dogs.

Maybe it wasn't only because of that, the two dogs. A M. Fouillerot enters the picture. Now he was somebody. He even took the trouble to go to the *gendarmerie* in person. He wanted to know, first, if it was certain that the corpse was really that of Dupuis, called Bouscarle. It was certain. It still lacked the head, which had become detached during the ramble on the mountain-tops; they looked for it, but as the two dogs belonged to Bouscarle and the belt to which they were tied was Bouscarle's, the body encircled by this belt was very probably that of the aforesaid.

Fouillerot, then, or, more exactly, M. Fouillerot, announced that Jules Dupuis, called Bouscarle, was the owner of more than a million in treasury bonds. This was in 1934, you can imagine the sensation! It was necessary to begin all over again, just when everything had been settled. Bouscarle had gone to Omergues, that was proved, he had been seen. He had soaked it up all day, mixing white and red, that was established, there were those available who had drunk with him; during the night he had decided to climb back to his own place, he had succumbed to the cold and had died; the dogs had dragged him. As if Bouscarle could succumb to anything, even when he was as tight as an owl! But an autopsy is an autopsy, and facts are facts. Only—a million, that's a fact too. And where was it, this million?

And, to begin with, who was Fouillerot, M. Fouillerot? There one was on solid ground. Fouillerot was a retired process-server who had exercised his talents over at Draguignan. After making his pile (a modest one) he had returned to the district, for he was a native. He had bought a small estate a few kilometres from Revest and after two or three years of . . . conversations, investigations, standing coffees, he had begun to lend money right and left, first at a small annual interest, then larger, then larger still and by the month. For the most part this worked well. He was also an agent for the banks, and in this capacity he cashed drafts and bought securities. That's how he knew about Bouscarle's fortune in treasury bonds. It was he who had sold him the State-guaranteed bonds. And he took the credit for it.

To begin with, they went over Bouscarle's house with a fine-tooth comb. Not a job for the squeamish. They found rats, decayed fox-pelts, ancient cheeses and, on top of this, an Olibet biscuit-tin containing forty gold pieces.

The million seemed within reach. But, in the event, nothing more was found; and yet God knows that the discovery of the gold pieces had given everybody ideas. It was even necessary to post a *gendarme* on watch at night.

Fouillerot, or rather M. Fouillerot, suggested that Bouscarle must have been in the habit of carrying his fortune on his person. He did make it clear that these bonds were large coupons which could very easily be kept in a coat or trouser-pocket, or in a special pocket. Then people were suddenly reminded of the coat of the col du Négron. In fact, people thought of a lot of things, all at the same time. They thought of the coat, they thought of Martin, they thought of Siméon, they thought of exhuming Bouscarle.

Nothing in the coat, which was at the *gendarmerie*. But someone might have got there first. Martin? No, he'd been at home with a broken leg for three weeks. Siméon? No, you only needed to glance at the lad, he was capable of killing a monster but not of putting his hand on a rotting corpse. And what for, anyway? Besides Fouillerot, no one knew of the existence of this million.

A moment! That might be something! And yet, taking everything into account: no, since it was Fouillerot who had talked, and, further, he had just given the *gendarmerie* the numbers of the treasury bonds so that a stop might be placed on them. And anyway, what was a million to M. Fouillerot, who had the whole of the High Country as his milch cow?

Time passes, summer comes, storms break, the rain

falls, the animals multiply—foxes, badgers, stone-martens, weasels (I'm thinking of Bouscarle's head that hasn't been found yet), and rodents of every species from the squirrel to the shrew, not forgetting the rat; it's unlikely that a treasury bond, even in big bills, can survive all that. Only the Dupuis-Melchiors' mouths still water a bit for this million, the others have lost their appetite. And then they say : 'Who knows? Perhaps he didn't have a million after all. This Fouillerot always plays a queer game, who knows but this time too he's not leading everyone up the garden path?'

So far, it's a superficial civilization one sees. Everything seems to take place, as nearly as possible, just as in the Low Country or anywhere else. There are the *gendarmes*, there are even the numbers of the treasury bonds, which are enjoined against, as it might be in Paris or Romorantin. There has even been an autopsy, rudimentary I agree, since it was performed by a local doctor little used to forensic discipline; the exact date, and still more the exact time, of his death were not determined, but how could they have been?

Bouscarle was in pretty bad shape after having been dragged through the thickets by the watchdogs attached to his person. Finally, the Dupuis-Melchiors plead a distant cousinship to claim the inheritance, and at least the forty louis (though the State claims thirty-nine of these). Bouscarle is buried (twice). The dogs are buried. Things go their customary way.

In the course of this History and Geography of the High Country one may have the opportunity to spy furtively the colour of the cards, the underneath side, where there is no longer any image of civilization. Assuredly, the whole game won't be displayed; but Ennemonde, the Dupuis-Melchiors, this Fouillerot, perhaps even the widow with the flag, here are the elements for an enquiry and he who seeks finds (not always what he wants, here less than anywhere). And there are not only these; there are those who will cross their path, or those who have already crossed it and turn back or go straight on. What is sure is that it's not a matter of conversation but of action; here one says little but does much. One seems to be sleeping or dreaming, resting on a stick or moving very slowly; at last one strikes some damned flint and some fine sparks fly.

In connection with the heart (its absence, as we mentioned earlier) there are two persons in need of attention. First, Bouscarle himself and next, little Siméon. Bouscarle was seventy when he died; sixty-nine and three months to be exact. The million had caused amazement because of the mere sound of the word. For Bouscarle might well have had a million; if he had sold his entire stock of lavender essence he might have had even more. He had sold a part of this stock, quite a large part, to a buyer from Grasse who came forward; what he had not sold was not recovered. But look : the State has taken thirty-nine of the forty louis; the Melchiors have no desire to continue fattening the tax-collector at that rate, so whatever one has or hasn't found, there's no point to it, for how can one supervise any sealing of property on the gloomy slopes at Pompe, or anything else? The frost and snow will crack the wax or the wind will blow in the doors, and then it takes a good day's journey on foot to go and check things. Good; there's a parenthesis to give some consistence to this million that was of no use on the slopes. Let us return to Bouscarle.

Seventy years old. He'd never been a colossus. A metre, seventy-five in his prime. For ten years he had lived with two dogs fastened to his belt. First he had two red ones, then one died and he had one red and one black. The ones who dragged him about and partly devoured his guts were two great German shepherd-dogs. For ten years Bouscarle walked and slept tied to two dogs. When he went for a drink the dogs crouched beside him. With a word, even less, with a click of the tongue, he could launch them at the throat of no matter whom. What was he afraid of to reach this condition? Of being robbed? No, the rifle he carried like everyone else was sufficient guarantee against theft; he did not fear Martin, from Montbrun; it became known event-ually that after having given each other a drubbing they had become good friends, as often happens, and that they had even sometimes accompanied each other (plus the two dogs) for some minor nocturnal debaucheries at the widow's with the flag, who sold wine on the quiet.

The way in which the people here have for centuries sited their houses always surprises strangers. They are never in front of a good view; and the places called Bellevue (and they are many) are always uninhabited. One might think that if they bury their dwellings in the most sunken valleys, in places, sometimes, where the sun never penetrates, it's to shelter from the wind. Now, once one has got to know these people at all, it's apparent that they love the wind to distraction and that they'd even pay to have wind. They've no need to pay, they've got it, solidly and permanently. So it isn't because of the wind that they hide themselves, it's to suppress, as far as possible, whatever outdoes them, and when I say outdoes, I mean in height.

When they are at home and look out of the window, or when they're outside about the building, everything is the height of a man, even the tallest beeches, which one can always climb and, if need be, dwell in as the famous Numa Pellisson did. So no problems of identity, there is an awareness of self. This one no longer has when one is on the heights; and one is obliged to go there thousands of times in a lifetime, often to go very early—like Siméon, for instance, who is only fourteen—and sometimes to stay there for a long time.

As one climbs the hardiest oaks, the tallest beeches disappear after having stooped to one's feet. There is a moment when the treetops touch the soles of one's shoes, then the horizon spreads out. And Christianity effaces itself. As God, so one says, has created his enemies, so he has created this landscape. That which undoes the hearts of men is never terrible; on the contrary it readily accords with peace and beauty. From Mont Viso, that is to say from Italy, to the Gerbier-des-Joncs and beyond, even as far as the black cliffs of the Margeride, that is to say as far as the Auvergne; and from Mont Blanc, which appears very high up in the north like a veiled mirror, as far as Sainte-Victoire which sails full south with all canvas set, and even, through the gap that separates Sainte-Victoire from Mont Apollon, as far as the sea, whose fine foamy curve one can espy: these are the two diameters. All round the circumference of the circle, starting in the east and moving to the south, there are, first, the great Alpes du Briançonnais—le Pelvoux with its snow and its Écrins, then le Queyras with le Viso—in front of which there advance les Alpes du Gapençais, le Dauphiné d'Orcières, then a little farther forward still, les Alpes de Digne and Barcelonnette, the Basses Alpes so-called, contrary to reality. The latter are linked with nearer massifs, while the great peaks fly towards the Italian frontier—the mountains of Castellane, le Mourre de Chanier, the Mont Aiguines that descends gently to the plateaux of the Haut-Var. In winter one can see the spread of the shimmering red of its great oak forests and, in summer, the wine-blue of oceans of great depth. Finally there emerges Mont Apollon, which has two heads, then a peaked cliff that the uninformed take for the Sainte-Victoire but is the Sainte-Baume, then Sainte-Victoire, but in between, above the fields of Pourrières, where the Cymbri and the Teutons were wiped out, one can see the sea. Moving on, to those regions between south and west where, in the afternoons, a kind of luminous haze always smokes, the sky strives to touch the lowlands of la Crau, of the Camargue, and the marshes of the Golfe du Lion. On this aspect, then, there is not the smallest mountain; but often, at the most unexpected moment, in fine calm weather for instance, a strange colour is to be seen. It is a kind of black in which reflections shimmer. Sometimes it is as if the Andes or the Himalayas loom up with their shadows; at other times it may resemble the sea pressed against a

28

wall; in fact, it is the light devouring itself and, being devoured, leaving in its place this abyss which is not even cosmic. This ferocity of the light arises from the incessant movement of the reflections of the troubled sea in front of Port-Saint-Louis-du-Rhône and the Saintes-Maries, magnified by the great glass lens of the Vaccarès and the dazzling vapours the sun sucks from the lands embraced by the Rhône. The stony hills of Nîmes do not escape this furnace; they can be seen only in the morning, with the sun at one's back. And in spring they appear as if salt-encrusted because of the cistus flowers. At the limits of these lands of light the rustic mountains of the Lozère begin to rear themselves: le Branoux which dominates Alès, l'Aigoual which is flanked by le Causse Noire, le Méjean which dominates Florac, le Lozère which dominates Mende and, farthest of all, l'Aubrac which looks from here like a patch of old lichen. It is in these mountains that the sun sets in summer. But as it sinks over them it abolishes, it obliterates them, and it is over towards the north that it kindles its fires—in the Auvergne, Mont Murat, Mont Margeride, that stays an acid green all summer despite its distance, Monts Alègre, de la Chaise-Dieu, Pilatus; and suddenly, beyond Pilatus, a corner of the horizon which is quite empty, the valley through which the Rhône descends. Beyond, one must look very high up to perceive the gleam of Mont Blanc, then the mountains of the Dauphiné come to cling to those of the Briançonnais and the circle of the spiked trap is closed once more.

If, from the peak of the Gondrand that dominates

Mont Genèvre, one takes a few steps in the direction of l'Infernet, one can see in the distance, towards Marseilles, between Monts d'Embrun and le Queyras, a white crest; this is the High Country. If from Toulon, one travels towards the valley of the Gapeau, taking the road from Solliès-Pont to Brignoles, when one has flanked the massif of the Sainte-Baume and has reached the intersection with the road to Saint-Maximin, it takes perhaps some twenty metres to the right of the path to reach a fine cherry-tree, and looking towards the north one sees in the sky a small white triangle: this is the High Country. It can be seen from the road from Saint-Flour to Le Puy, just as one begins the descent to Langeac, shortly after having passed Pinols; it is in the east, like a cloud. On the other hand, if one comes from Paris by car, or on the train, one will never see it; after Valence it is hidden by the mountains of the Drôme, after Orange masked by le Ventoux, after Avignon obliterated by the light.

In summer as in winter, from all these dreadful distances, it appears white. Naturally, in the winter this is snow. But the winter is not the season most to be feared in the High Country, the summer there claims many more victims. It is an error to suppose that Jesus Christ has replaced everything, that's obvious up here. The snow is nothing, even ranged by the wind in drifts ten metres high, even when in storms it engulfs fathers of families returning from earning their daily bread. A man born in these parts, brought up in these forests, following his trade in these heights, is unheeding of the Christian hell. The concept of sin is completely at variance with the compass-card. If he wants to live he must sin, every day, every hour, and even invent sins a thousand times more mortal than the notorious ones are supposed to be. He must turn them into a personal arsenal, mark them with his own cipher, utilize them in his own manner, which is the only way to use them properly and with full efficacity. The New Testament suits no one, the Old a few, sometimes, but everyone is in accord with the sentiment (which has no name in any language) that everything is only dust. Starting from that, only individuals are possible and the heart useless, or a nuisance, like the Amazon's breast. Its ablation is self-inflicted at a very early date, well before Matriculation.

Summer is sparkling and brief. It tears itself out of spring in five days, it blossoms in twenty, its death-throes take ten, and then it is autumn. Near every shepherd's hut there is a cherry-tree; sometimes it's been planted, often it has planted itself. It has nothing in common with the cherries of the plain or the valleys. It is generally a tree very low on the ground with an enormous trunk exuding golden resin through every scar on its bark. Its branches are poorly developed by reason of their constant struggle against the winds, and bear small leaves and miniature fruits, hardly bigger than redcurrants, which redden at the end of July. At this time the season has hardly shaken loose from spring; its white dust is still suspended in the morning light; but all at once noontide is heavy and the evenings lengthen out indefinitely into red until the appearance of the first star. The air suddenly becomes edible. No one who has not breathed it can appreciate the meaning of this word. The lung becomes a sense-organ. It is not a matter of odour or freshness, but of chemical quality (like that of jugged hare). For a very long moment it seems that all motion has become purposeless, so no more noise. From the smallest insect to the largest quadruped nothing moves unless it is absolutely necessary, it is enough to breathe; this breathing brings an unparalleled joy which satisfies even the insatiable curiosity of men. Yes, it really seems that even the appetite for knowledge is appeased, merely by virtue of distending oneself with air. The bees are the first to recover and to realize that, on the contrary, it's necessary to get a move on, then the birds: first the hawfinches which feed on the seeds of the miserable alfalfa that covers the steppes, with their clumsy, monotonous song; the warblers, carnivorous and cruel, first execute their arabesques to explore the sky from ground-level up to where the lark already quivers, then express themselves in short febrile songs like cries; last, the heavy birds of prey fly up from the grass where they were sleeping.

It is a carrion season. The sheep panic easily in the clear mornings. The bees follow the tracks of little reptilian creatures, of ferrets, stoats, weasels and martens, in the hope of being able to relish some freshly-spilt blood or some putrescence with which to joyfully manufacture their sugar. They accumulate hundredweights of black sulphur-smelling honey in the trunks of dead trees. Its weight is such that the wood of these trees, dried up by sun and wind, often splits apart and the honey is shed, while the fury of millions of bees sets the sky ablaze. Events of this nature are not rare, but they stand out in isolation. In 1927 the oldest Bernard son, who did not get away in time, was kept imprisoned in his shepherd's hut for a week. On the second day this oldest (Kléber) succeeded in setting his flock free. Sheep are not much afraid of bee-stings, except on the muzzle, and even then they begin to secrete an acid mucus that protects them while the bees, on the other hand, stay imprisoned in the fleece. Kléber knew this and banked on it to some extent. The flock carried off a fair number of the warriors but some remained who maintained a sort of to-and-fro and summoned reinforcements. The oldest son still can't speak of it without a tremor. He felt overpowered, he, a chap who even then already weighed his hundred kilos, unable to do anything against them. And no deliverance was at hand either. When the Bernard family saw the sheep arrive they understood, but what to do? They tried to climb up to the hut but, a kilometre away, just as they topped the brow towards the down-slope, they heard the rumbling and saw, down there in front of them, a house which had lost its shape and its angles and was now only a rounded mass of bees. There may very well have been one or two bee-keepers there and even one, so it was said, who could charm bees and had posed for a photograph showing him with a swarm clinging to his cheeks and hanging from his chin like a beard, but this was a little beyond his mark. He didn't believe his eyes, he said, but he preferred to believe them rather than go and look more closely. Someone thought of the army's flamethrowers and the town hall telephoned to

33

Digne, who telephoned to Avignon, but there weren't any flamethrowers. At the Engineers' at Avignon someone suggested firemen as an alternative. But what to do with the firemen? What could they pump in this country where water is scarcer than wine? Besides, throwing water on bees (on these bees) was . . . but I owe you too much respect! Surely, however, the elder son could not be left in this situation? But he was so left. At last, four or five days later, he arrived one morning trembling like a leaf. What had happened? He knew nothing about it. All he could say was that that night, unlike the other nights, there had not been that incessant darting against the window-panes, nor the buzzing that went on in the chimney, despite the fire of hell that he never stopped stoking. He went to see; the window-panes were clear and he could 'see the stars again'. None the less, he kept on his guard. With the dawn he realized that the siege was raised. He opened the door, he threw a few stones into the grass, ready to shut himself in again if it was a matter of an ambush, but no, they had departed. He made his way towards the valleys.

Thus he was not delivered, they delivered him, they abandoned him to his sad fate. Because of it he retained a wound to his pride, like someone who has been treated with contempt. Nor could he understand why no one had come to his aid. His father told him that it was because he did not want to understand. But that was exactly what he did want, he was not the odd wheel of the cart in the family, he was the oldest and he wanted to know why he had been abandoned. It was useless to repeat that it was not a question of knowing, but a question of understanding, and that to understand he must put himself in their place. It was impossible to make him admit that his place had not been the worst.

Talking with the oldest Bernard boy nowadays or discussing some matter, it's always necessary to be a bit careful, his repartees are sometimes difficult to tolerate. He is married, he even has a pretty little daughter. His is not a frank gaze, he seems to be weighing you up mentally, to calculate; what can he be calculating?

As far as he is concerned, the bees that were besieging him must have received an order to abandon him. They can often be seen to receive orders. They don't rage all the time. They are never very well behaved but one can get on with them well enough provided one allows oneself no familiarity and always gives ground. Over at Larrau there are some twenty dead oaks; these are very big trees that have been struck by lightning one after the other during the course of the last thirty years. First they gradually lost their upper branches, then their bark fell away and they were left white as ivory. It is astonishing when one approaches to hear them murmuring despite everything. Stop at once : those are bees. This is the biggest concentration of wild bees in the whole region. In the sixteenth century there was a similar one, perhaps even bigger, fifty kilometres to the west of here at the entrance to the gorges of the Nesque, at the place now called le rocher de Cire.

The trunks are a good two or three metres round, seven to eight high, and stuffed to the brim with black honey smelling slightly of sulphur and innumerable battalions, republics and other mass organizations.

Political commandos fly off from here and go to disorganize, pervert, bribe, subvert and finally lead away the peaceful population of the apiaries maintained by several of the farms. These expeditions can be seen crossing the steppe like light grey clouds. Obviously, it's best not to be in their path but if by chance this is unavoidable, one does not run much risk. These expeditions have a purely political orientation and must be composed of orators rather than warriors. It's enough, should you find yourself face to face with one of them, not to run away and not to thrash your arms about; if you keep still there is no danger.

This is not the case at the approaches to the lightning-struck forest. The bees have drawn a frontier round their metropolis which may not be crossed. There is nothing to indicate this frontier. It is of air, and in the air, but if you want to recognize it, cross it. Cross it, be it understood, with the greatest caution, step by step, and ready to turn back at the slightest warning, which is not slow to come; as soon as you have crossed the imaginary line, beyond which the bees consider that you are on their territory, torrents of warriors hurl themselves at you. Turn back, go home, they won't follow you, they stay for a while in suspense at the limit of their territory; they wait; if you don't persist they return to their barracks, squadron by squadron. Do the same ten times, they will do the same ten times over in exactly the same way.

The angry buzzing of the charging warriors is terrifying. It is a noise like thunder, I mean that it is of the same quality. It produces simultaneously the same awful satisfaction of the ear and the same agitation of the heart. On reflection, it is much more disturbing than the sound of thunder. Like that, it is cosmic; yet it is produced simply by the insects scratching their bellies to show their anger. Thus Zeus and the God of Abraham are not more firmly anchored in the world than this little blonde fly; it's enough for him to be a million or two strong and to scratch his belly with claws a tenth of a millimetre long for his anger to be measured by infinite space. There remains the God of Cromwell : he stands the comparison.

Another peculiarity of the summer is that it is the proving-ground of the passions. No hate, no ambition, no jealousy, no love but succeeds in giving battle during this delicate little month. The love affairs are only there for the record, it's simple for them and soon over : the girls conceive in August (the married women in January). These conceptions do not usually result from a free gift of the self, rather from a kind of ram-ewe mating. There are exceptions : one of the Rupert-Calicots conceived in August. However, she had pretty well passed the brunt of the storm, it was her fourth child. Her husband gave the impression of finding it natural enough. He deceived no one. The son born of this conception never received the consideration that was given his brothers and sisters, people still look around. Sometimes one says to oneself : Perhaps so-and-so? and for six months one imagines and finds resemblances. Then they are there no more and one passes on to someone else. The boy is taciturn and even in his relations with his family there is a little something,

37

which he derives from his own authority.

It will end up all right. Hatred, suspicion, jealousy are products of this country. If one has no time to waste on love, one can amuse oneself with these. It isn't that these people are any worse than others, it's just that, as extreme individualists and irremediably solitary, they are always afraid of being duped; now, if love often makes them dupes, hate never does so, there one is on solid ground. I love you, that's never certain, it demands proof; I hate you, that's solid gold. It should not be deduced that this is a kind of Far West, a misunderstanding whose origin might be ascribed to the fact that firearms are much in use and to the nature of the country. Well before the Americans had discovered that the West is far off, this country already behaved like ancient China. Hate does not kill here, it plays billiards; people who hate one another seem to have a mutual attachment, and in fact they do. They are often seen together, one might almost say always. On many occasions they bill and coo; they go as far as to help each other. This is the opposite to the Montagues and Capulets. If they should meet in the wilderness nothing will happen, or if anything does happen it will be well-behaved. One will do his utmost and even risk his own skin for the other. And of course there are marriages between families that hate each other, many in fact. If there were no marriages one might sometimes find oneself in difficulty. There is marriage, there is frequentation, there is often association, there is cohabitation and that the purest form of hate, without the least flaw, tempered in spring water, sharpened and cutting like a razor. So what, you may ask? So the blows are delivered from very far off and take a great deal of time to arrive and through many interposed individuals. When the blow falls, one would swear that God had wielded the axe. It's not here that revolvers dangle on the thigh, nests feathered behind a quickness of draw superior to that of one's enemies. No, it's more common to have a sleepy air, to turn the tongue seven times in the cheek —but the word that is finally pronounced does for a whole family, sometimes an entire generation. Someone has gone to utter this word dozens, even hundreds, of kilometres away, in offices, to petty tradesmen, men of law, men of affairs, county councillors, deputies, senators, tax inspectors, fee-collectors, anyone with an ounce of power, anyone who makes birdlime, traps for foxes, snares of iron wire, pitfalls, anyone concerned with offices, expenses, promenades along endless corridors, insomnia, jangled nerves. Someone makes use of the oldest daughter, the youngest, the wife, party or religion (or, more exactly, the Church). Once this game has been set on foot, the whole political, financial, administrative, judicial, legal, penitential and outside broking apparatus of the Department and neighbouring Departments is sensitized to a degree, it becomes agitated and snaps its jaws for a word, a conjunction, a simple comma, sometimes a silence. It devours fields, sheepfolds, flocks, farmyards, cupboards, chests and even people (when the ploy is really successful).

The manoeuvres necessary to set this machinery in motion take place in summer. Or in the depths of a factitious night. It is, in fact, a matter of concealing the deeds and gestures of hate in action. Everyone is on the lookout; the roads are empty; if Ferdinand is seen boarding the coach, where's he off to? If one branch of the Dupuis has been nicknamed Automobile it is because in 1907 Dupuis *père* ruined his daughter-in-law through getting himself judiciously conveyed by the car of M. Auriol Joséphin, the wood merchant of Montbrun. This was one of the first cars to be seen and it was the first time that one of these modern devices was employed for these civilizing purposes in the region. More recently, if the last of the Cicérons (his two brothers are dead, one died naturally, the other of a tropical sore on the nose) is called Cicéron-Clarinette, it is because he tricked everyone by leaving his wireless set on while he went to Forcalquier to split on the traffic of Bonardi, the Piedmontese (called Biribi, no one knows why). Traffic in alcohol, ostensibly, false of course, but with traffic in alcohol one's on velvet. There's searching, probing everywhere, everything is set on fire or made to bleed, the house, stables, cowsheds, sheepfold and barns are completely ransacked; when they've finished a sow couldn't find her little ones. If nothing's unearthed that's perfect, once they've got the flea in their ear they'll come back and start all over again. This is one of the most spectacular ruins there is, agreeable to contemplate, and in stages. Of course, Bonardi didn't take it lying down, he was not an Italian for nothing, but that's not the point just now.

We have passed over the matter of love too quickly. As far as the uses the young make of it go, there's no need to repeat what has been said. It may be that chance will reveal a couple who regard each other fondly, holding each other by the little finger, but don't put too much store in fondness, it's a deception, it's only there from tradition; they are simply quiet persons who take things slowly, but at the end of their little jaunt it's the same as for the others, they come a cropper. On the other hand the countryside is full of many a Philemon and Baucis. Their story is a little outside a description of the summer. Take, for instance, Titus the Long and Camille.

Twenty years ago I often used to wander over this countryside in every direction. It reminded me of the Scottish moors, for which I'd retained some nostalgia. I took up quarters in a solitary pub, miles from any place of habitation. It was a simple little shepherd's hut where tracks intersected, where the traveller could find a glass of beer or wine if he needed it. In addition I had some fairly good grub, ranging from thrush and plover to sausage with cabbage, and a paillasse in an outhouse. Camille, who kept this pub, was an old friend, she was seventy-two at that time but green as a bay-tree. In her youth she had been the prettiest of women, the most beautiful of the entire region. Nothing remained of this but an extraordinary head of jade-black hair without a single white hair. She had not married and lived alone.

I arrived at her place without warning. Five times out of ten I'd find every door open and no one answered my calls. I knew the drill, I went down to the cowshed and found my Camille there, dead drunk, unconscious, lying under the cows' feet in the dung and piss. She was a corpulent person. I confined myself (in any case it was all it was possible to do) to dragging her by the leg well away from the animals. After that I followed the routine; I would go up to her room and, if it was daytime, I'd hang a white cloth on the fastener of the shutters, or if it was dusk or night I'd light a candle or a petrol-lamp and stand it behind the window-pane. There was nothing left but to wait.

It was necessary to wait an hour, and in bad weather much longer. The man who would come from far off was no longer young—Titus, known as the Long, seventy-eight at the time. He would answer the call no matter what the weather. Once, it was in a wind fit to drag the horns from an ox, the expression is not too strong, he covered the last hundred yards on all fours, having been blown over more than ten times on the way. He would arrive, see me, and understand at once. Together, we could carry Camille and get her up to her room. He always took the head and I the legs. We laid the drunken woman on the floor and went down to the kitchen to heat some water; when the water was hot I helped Titus to carry up the kettle, the bucket and the soap. After that I left him alone, it was his affair. He did not call me until he had washed Camille from head to foot and changed her into clean linen. We exerted ourselves again (it took all our strength) to lift the corpulent old lady. She was so far gone that she didn't wake up even while all this was going on. At most she groaned. He tucked her in and we returned to the kitchen.

Titus and I used to have long conversations. He had been nicknamed the Long, not because of his height—

he was not tall, stocky rather with his head buried in his shoulders—but because it took him an infinite time to get anything done. What an unskilled man could do in two hours he, though very skilful at everything, would take two days over. And so with all else. He was the son of Titus the One-armed. This one-armed man had two arms. He had gained his nickname by always wearing his coat over his shoulders without ever pulling on the sleeves, which swung empty on either side of him; hence the One-armed, that's all there was to it. This armless man had married a money-bag : Léa, the only daughter of the Romualds, well-known for being both uncivilized and the owners of a fine farm at Roquette. The One-armed had two children by Léa : the elder, a girl, Adonise, and the younger, our famous Titus the Long. When the One-armed died, Adonise had already been married to Paul-Émile, the grocer at Banon, for five years. There was an arrangement between brother and sister over Roquette that Titus should work it alone. He never married. Léa died soon after.

Roquette is an important farm : sheepfolds for a hundred or so sheep, vast stables with mangers for more than six horses, barns to match, living quarters with at least twenty to twenty-five rooms or alcoves, and a number of hectares that didn't amount to much, being purely and simply wild, but with woods one could draw on if need be. 'The Long' camped out in a ground-floor room, he limited his exploitation to what he could manage single-handed, and finally he contented himself with the resources he derived from raising fifty ewes; it should be said that within a few years he had become

43

a pastmaster in the art of living in a closed economy.

This was the period when Camille, five kilometres away, was in the flower of her springtime. She was not married either, at least not before the Mayor. Camille's life had been exceptional. She preferred her freedom to family life. In a region where the most virile surround themselves with a thousand wooden fortifications this is a decision more heroic than that of the Cid Campéador. Her character shone forth in the blue (it could only be called adamantine) of her eyes and the raven's-wing hair that stayed pure black until extreme old age. Beautiful, well-made, and well-made by the peasant canons that demand something of answering solidity, she was pretty as well, that is by ordinary human standards. She had many gallants. She did not let those she chose languish. Her choice might be extravagant; there was a scandal at one time which I won't go into, but which disturbed even the bishopric. Distracted by mentioning her beauty and its consequences, I've forgotten to mention that Camille, orphaned at at early age, was brought up by an uncle who probably taught her a thing or two when the time arrived, and who finally left her the inheritance of a good share of his estate. She did not need to worry over-much about the future; provided, of course, she led the life people lead here. This did not bother her; she knew how to live humbly except as far as her freedom was concerned. She could live for months on oil, salt and bread, provided she could indulge in the good times she enjoyed.

From the first of my conversations with Titus the Long he did not conceal from me that he had loved

Camille for over sixty years. He also declared immediately that he had, 'never asked for anything and never received anything'. This was not from timidity. When the men used to fight over Camille he went to fight too; but when he won (which happened three times) he returned to Roquette. He let the loser have the benefit, if he was still capable of it. For these were real masculine encounters. One Easter Sunday they did their best to break his arm; one evening he was suddenly attacked by some woodmen a few hundred yards from his home and left for dead, with arms spreadeagled, in his yard, but he remembered the heads he had broken, especially at the time of the scandal. He confessed to me that he could gladly have killed someone then. The favourite was less mettlesome and did not take part in the fights. These males fought each other then for Camille as men used to fight for the Tsar. Then the less mettlesome fellow was transferred to another parish and Camille's gallants continued their former sentry-guard.

Pride, evidently, on the part of Titus the Long. At Saumanes he met one of his cousins, a former colonial sergeant. He taught him a few tricks, notably how to use his feet; a sort of footwork, part bayonet fencing, part boxing, part what-you-will, that worked wonders. His feet came into action at the precise moment and damaged exactly what needed to be damaged. It was overpoweringly efficient. He began to be feared. He did not create a void round Camille because as soon as his back was turned someone jumped into her bed, and he knew it. He fought to fight : pride.

It does seem that at the time of all these battles Titus

had pitched the love he bore Camille at a phenomenal height. Maybe he lied to himself, but he remained faithful to his lie. When his lower parts plagued him too much he went to pay a visit to the widow with the tricolour flag. His sister tried to marry him off. He resisted, she insisted; she came to cluck at Roquette. Such a large house was intended for a family. She had a choice of girls to hand, some not bad and with prospects. Titus soon went about reducing the farm buildings to his own size. He removed four-fifths of the roofing, leaving only what was above the room he lived in. The bad weather was responsible for turning the rest into a ruin within a few months. Elders and nettles invaded the room where Titus the Long had been born and the one where Titus the One-armed had died. There, that shows how proud he was.

Was he jealous? When I put the question he chewed his moustache for a long time. Yes. And one day he decided to go to Marseilles. You might as well say the Antipodes! An hour on foot, three hours in a bus, four hours by train. Why Marseilles? Because he wanted to buy a telescope. Not field-glasses; a telescope that would fold up like the one to be seen in the hands of Admiral Villeneuve at the Battle of Trafalgar (he had the picture at home). One day he showed me what he still called, using the old-fashioned expression, his 'spy-glass'. It was a magnificent instrument, as good as new, he had looked after it so carefully; it must have cost the eyes out of his head. Folded, it lived in a round leather box that could be carried on a shoulder-strap.

At first, he could not see Camille's house from

Roquette, he had to climb a beech to see over the coppices. He would have spent his days in the beech. He undertook to clear a cutting in the brush. The brush, that's white oak. He took months over this work. He cut down trees over a breadth of three yards and straight towards his goal, the way one routes a power-line through a forest nowadays. Thus he no longer needed to climb the beech. He could keep an eye on Camille while staying seated in front of the door of his house in the summer, and beside his hearth in winter. Though this keeping an eye on her was gratuitous now; the time of the battles was past; Camille's visitors came in good order and all honour. Titus confined himself to counting the visitors through his telescope which, so he told me, did not make him suffer over-much. I tried to understand this indifference. It is self-explanatory. During our conversations round the stove, while Camille was sleeping off her wine between the white sheets, Titus often repeated to me : 'No one could take her away from me. You see! I've got her and I'll keep her.'

He does not see her as she really is. He sees her as he wants her to be. Neither the beautiful brunette nor the poor drunkard. The beautiful brunette was impossible to keep on a leash, even with rifle-shots; or to manage this, it would be she he had to fire on. Titus is not one of those who kill what they love (as it is generally agreed that everyone does more or less). The country here is so poor that no one destroys anything, neither what one loves nor what one detests; everything is kept, good and bad, for who knows, one fine day one may need everything. He came to terms. Through Camille he experi-

47

enced joy and suffering; suffering to have joy, joy to have suffering, and it was so well arranged that it occupied his entire life. He does not see the poor drunken woman as she is, rolling in her piss, because at that very moment he knows that, with hot water, clean sheets, fresh linen and love, he will turn her into what he wants her to be. And no one can take her away from him any more. Had anyone ever taken her away from him?

The forest ride, the spy-glass alley that he had cut in the woods over forty years ago, has been carefully maintained; nothing obstructs the view of Camille's house from Roquette. At Roquette, on the window-ledge, a little wooden-framed base supports the telescope. It's not there to count the swains any longer, it's to watch for the appearance of the white rag at the shutter-fastener or the light of the lamp behind the panes. I continue to speak of it in the present, and yet it will soon be three years since the grandson of Adonise and Paul-Émile removed the spy-glass. Fortunately, Titus died in the fine weather so that he was found right away by the shepherd of Villard. Camille died the next day. I had the brashness to ask of what; they answered (for they're not simpletons) that she had died of death. Which, on reflection, satisfied me. The spy-glass alley is filling up with new trees.

This is all very far from summer, of which we still have the night to describe; especially the moonless night. Nothing is darker, nothing more glowing. There are so many stars, they are so sharp, so neat, so well polished by the glass wind that they give a sort of light.

In reality it is not a light (it's even the opposite), it is a golden powder with which they cover every object and every shape. Sunlight or moonlight, which is its reflection, casts shadows; the phosphorescence of the stars casts no shadow; it evokes the appearance of the world by dusting it, not by lighting it, it does not come from a particular spot in the heavens like the sun's rays or the moon's reflection, it comes from every quarter of the sky at once; it illuminates both the front and the back of objects at the same. time and with the same light, it falls from everywhere at once, like rain.

These nights are not relaxing, they are disturbing. They do not tell of the intermittent disappearance of the sun but of its final disappearance. The world is sunless, but there's no telling that it will return; it even says that it will not return. There's no need to be a great scholar to understand this, such a night can only be there for ever. And, even though one knows the sun will return, the most essential part of the soul, the most ancient, indulges itself in imagining that it doesn't know. It is a game at which simple souls are pastmasters. They substitute the anxieties of the primitive world for the anxieties of civilization.

In the villages, in the farms, some of which are the size of villages, they sometimes take chairs out to the thresholds of the houses on summer evenings. They take the air. The air still has an exquisite quality like spring water. But as soon as night posts its great constellations above the street or above the courtyard, they go indoors and barricade the door. The rifle is useless, only sleep avails; or perhaps a certain kind of passion. And here we return to Ennemonde.

Surprising as it may be, one must remember that the High Country is not very large. From west to east, that is from the valley that separates le Ventoux from Lure to Sisteron, it measures about sixty-five kilometres; and from north to south, that is from the valley of the Jabron to Route Nationale 100, is a little more, say another fifteen or twenty kilometres. It includes only two townships, two villages, six hamlets of less than twenty inhabitants, and about fifty farms; in any case, all these inhabited places are adjacent to wild country. In so little space, and with so few people, one is bound to come across the same ones all the time. Especially since they are larger than life.

Honoré was still alive, but 'shrunk' to an extreme and kept on short commons at home. Ennemonde had taken possession of the rifle and her two oldest sons. She was no longer the ingenuous candidate for whatever might be 'normal' (even a school).* Above all, she was no longer the little infatuate of the glens of the col de la Croix. Fifteen years of a nightgown with a hole in it really settles a woman's spirit. Her body had become, by dint of repeated pregnancies, like the bodies of all the women of the High Country; it bore now only a remote relation to the human form. Her face was attractive despite the loss of all her teeth, since her lips were fleshy enough to remain full. She had a pretty pink complexion, her chestnut eyes were very limpid, without rings or wrinkles and with long curved lashes. Their

* An *école normale* is a teachers' training college.—Tr.

gaze was sometimes that of a young girl, more often not. She weighed over a hundred and thirty kilos but moved with surprising agility. The men joked about the thickness of her thighs, naturally without ever having seen them. Despite her weight and her gross limbs she was easily capable of covering twenty kilometres on foot in five hours, over difficult country. She had milk-white skin, having always protected it from the sun under hats, in long sleeves and high collars, like all those men and women who know what the sun is really like. She was not a woman to be readily explained. Those who saw her every day desired daily to penetrate her mystery; there was all that monstrosity, pictured as soft and milky, that moved under her skirts and the look in her fine eyes. This look counselled prudence; not that it was hostile; on the contrary.

In 1930 she bought a B 14 as a bargain, to visit the fairs. It was her oldest son, Samuel, who drove. The roads were not good. At the col de la Croix, where she had had her love affair with Honoré, the road was broken up by the feet of the sheep. If the trip took place at night or in cloud you had to strike the lamps with blows of your fist to get a little light. In fine weather, running downhill from there produced powerful sensations. Samuel remained cool, he was young, he had witnessed the success of his mother's *coup d'état*, after which nothing astonished him any more and he came down from the top at full tilt. Ennemonde enjoyed it.

The col de la Croix, the full title of which is the col de la Croix-de-l'Homme mort, gives access from the plateau to the lower ground to the north. If one looks closely, there are chasms on that side. They are not very obvious to anyone traversing the roads on foot because the lowlands are not overlooked from the bluffs and the eye has time to rest on the sharply sloping wooded plains. The pedestrian generally opines that there is a fine view on this route. In reality, towards Montbrun the ground falls seven hundred metres in level over five kilometres as the crow flies and, towards Les Fraissinières, the chasm is eight hundred metres deep. The road is cut out of friable shale. Even today, though tarred and supported by walls and edged with parapets, it is a headache for the highways department. It rapidly deteriorates, eroded by the frosts and thaws, oozings and tricklings of the spring. The folk of the High Country hardly use it and prefer to go round by Sault and Montbrun, adding fifty kilometres to their journey. Thirty years ago the road was maintained by the road-mender. Which is to say that during the summer he would saunter along there carrying a spade on his shoulder.

If anyone had told Ennemonde to go round by Sault, Montbrun, Barret, etc., on the grounds that the col de la Croix was blocked by bad weather, she would have replied that she hadn't a moment to lose. It was true. She was forty-one years old. She rushed headlong into the northern valleys as one rushes headlong into sin; like sin, they were gloomy, perfumed and full of under-growth. At the base of the slope the road entered tor-tuous passages. It intertwined with streams that were stony in the summer but could suddenly deepen into a spate of four or five metres after a storm. It brushed past odorous carpets of thyme, savory and lavender; it jostled against alders and willows smoking with pollen. It traversed shady paths of indescribable charm. Samuel, who stopped his engine at the col and free-wheeled right down the descent, stamping on the brake-pedal for all he was worth at the bends, amazed himself each time with the prodigious speed he attained in this downrush; he did not start his engine again until the first poplars of Fraissinières. As for Ennemonde, she was content to be swept along. It was magical. No question now of weight or bulk, she was a feather floating in the wind. The jolts did not precipitate her towards the abyss but towards the skies. For the first time she felt what it was to be intoxicated. According as to whether the bend threw her to left or right, Ennemonde would be leaning against the horizon above Montbrun as if to touch the setting sun or against the great glaciers of the Alps beyond which night was climbing. If the trip was in the morning she would lean to one side to brush her cheeks on the dawn winds, to the other to skim like a swallow above the mists that beset Montbrun. From time to time she would contemplate her fine Samuel who was driving; he also was quite detached from worldly cares, barely holding the steering-wheel with two fingers. If Honoré could have seen them, particularly if he could still have taken an interest in them, he would have said that these two were fixed fast in sin, easeful in sin, arrived in port in sin.

She managed her business affairs perfectly, did Ennemonde. The bargaining was haggled over to the last centime. Almost always she got the highest price. The brokers were not used to dealing with women—with widows sometimes, but widows are not women. She managed her household affairs perfectly, and her personal affairs; the latter without quite realizing it. She did not even know that she had had (for twenty years) a personal affair to see to and that she was in process of seeing to it.

After the hamlet of Fraissinières the road entered a defile between two walls of red rock. The passage of the B 14 stirred up clouds of crows in these depths. Leaving the defile one came out above a clearing carpeted with meadow-foxtail, strewn with Italian poplars and small gardens, in the midst of which there was coiled a sort of fortified town resembling a snail-shell, topped with an iron-capped steeple and surrounded by the boulevards where the fair was held.

This was a little agglomeration that had remained Huguenot for a long time, and had then gradually become worse. It was from places like these that the nightgown with a hole in it originated. No need to ferret about in the local haberdashers, it was enough to look at the shops and the bar-keepers. Everything here was mean and dirty, the people ate worms. The deep night that blew through the confusion of the valleys swept the streets without succeeding in ridding them of a stale biblical smell. The Protestants of these parts had protested against Protestantism from time immemorial. They had ended by worshipping no matter whom, provided that this no matter whom commanded intolerance. The crown of thorns was eaten in every home, at every meal. Religion was a sort of deal in which discomfort was always preferred to delight, contempt to pleasure, and, finally, vice to virtue.

The fair was held on the boulevards. This was an appropriate word here, where there really was a strip of open ground extending under the old ramparts. They were planted irregularly with a few wild acacias, Italian poplars, mulberries, elders, brambles and hawthorns. Hurdles enclosed small flocks brought for private sale. Ennemonde had no need to exhibit her animals. She was known, she was called 'la Grosse', it was recognized that she sold mutton of the first quality. She prowled about the fairground with Samuel at her heels and she did not wait to be approached by the buyers. She had fixed her price in advance and would not back down from it. At first there had been some attempt to inform her about current prices for meat and other nonsense, she took no notice so the sales were soon over; her price was either accepted or refused, there was no halfway house; if someone refused there was always someone else ready to accept.

After this she customarily treated herself to the table d'hôte, Samuel of course included. Samuel was her guardian angel. She looked at him with moist eyes. She would not let go of his arm. She pressed him against her. After the abysses of the road all these men had an intoxicating stink of goat. She felt herself threatened. It is just those most qualified for hell who most shirk its fires.

In 1932-3 people in these parts still lived as they had at the beginning of the century. The Hôtel Tilleuls where Ennemonde used to go had kept its traditions, one still ate at the table d'hôte and there was only one dish, from January 1st to New Year's Eve—*boeuf en daube*. It went on cooking without a break for 365 days and 365 nights in an enormous cauldron that hung in the dining-room hearth. The fire was only let out on the night of December 31st to January 1st, when the cauldron was emptied and cleaned and a start made with next year's *daube*; the fire was relit and hey presto! A *daube* to which hare and boar were added, as the hunt might allow, sometimes even fox, but carefully and only for the flavour.

It was a real table d'hôte; that is to say, the host himself presided, welcomed the guests and ate with them. As a rule he even joined in the conversation. Of course there was no question of this on fair days, just as there was no question of reserving places for the women on the *patron*'s right as he usually did. The service was equally simplified. On entering one passed in front of a sideboard where one took a bowl, that is a large soupplate, a fork and a knife and went and sat down at the table d'hôte, setting one's own place. There was soon brought a lump of bread weighing a kilo and a litre of wine and one could go and refill his plate at the stewpot. There was entitlement to a second bowl of stew but double price was charged for those who had replenishments of bread and wine, which was often the case.

This happened regularly with Samuel, who ate more than a kilo of bread at this meal; Ennemonde took her second bowl of *boeuf en daube* and drank her litre but never ate all her bread. She specially liked the rich golden-brown gravy of melted lard and fresh oil. She

56

used every time to take the precaution of bringing a soup-spoon with her, hidden in her corsage, and she would produce it at table to drink the gravy-like soup. Her iron-hard gums chewed the overcooked meat very well. It was a real blow-out. Doubly so; belly full, she risked mental separation from Samuel and even losing sight of him. She abandoned herself to a giddiness like that which had intoxicated her *en route*. She could see herself scandalizing this boring township. She no longer rubbed shoulders with clouds and heights, sunset and dawn, but with men stinking of goat.

One day after quitting the table she noticed a gathering by the Soubeyran gate, where they held the horse-market. She approached. It was a wrestler in clinging pink trunks standing on a carpet. He was challenging anyone to combat, specifying the Greco-Roman style of wrestling. He pointed to a red velvet cushion on which medals were pinned. One of these, according to him, was the White Elephant and had been awarded him by the King of Siam for having defeated a celebrated Chinese wrestler.

The finger that pointed at the bemedalled cushion intrigued Ennemonde, it was so enormous. Working back from the finger to the arm and from the arm to the rest of the body she was dazzled by a beauty that just suited her. He was a mass of fat and muscle, a metre sixty in height and a metre fifty broad; he had no neck. His head was planted directly on his shoulders, where it was held by a nape that bulged like an August melon. He had no eyes or nose or mouth worthy of the name. He seemed to breathe as a rock or a block of iron might

57

breathe, and it was equally surprising. Ennemonde began to breathe with his rhythm. She was fascinated by the man's hair-style; he was half-bald, with his hair greased with brilliantine and carefully combed with a parting on one side and a kiss-curl on his forehead.

She dreamed about him that night. She felt carried away. Oh, how marvellous he was!

She had to wait a month to find another fair. Ennemonde felt the time drag. She pictured the Greco-Roman again, straining against a blacksmith who had picked up the gauntlet. There was much more of a future in those muscles than in all the giddiness of the road. Vainly she trotted over the entire fairground; she could see no crowd and no wrestler. She searched till nightfall, when she had to go home.

The blacksmith who had wrestled kept a small garage on the boulevard where he sold agricultural machinery. Having passed twenty times in front of the forge where the man was working his bellows, she decided to go in and ask some questions. The recipient of the White Elephant was known everywhere as 'Clef-des-coeurs'; the blacksmith did not know his real name. He only came there when there was no more important fair somewhere else. It was very likely that he would be at Carpentras that day, where there was the sausage fair, the most popular of the year. Ennemonde's first thought was to go to Carpentras, although night had fallen. But there was Samuel. She had to go home.

She immediately consulted the almanack, even before saying good-evening. The next big fair was due to be held at Orange in a fortnight. It was a long way off.

Not so much the fourteen days, she had made up her mind, but Orange. She had never been there. She did not know the merchants there and they did not know her. And there was still Samuel. Something had to be done.

She did something. First, she learned to drive the B 14. She managed this at once; she had the Greco-Roman before her eyes. Then she took Samuel on one side and gave him a family talking-to. She was worshipped by her children. She gave her oldest a lecture, which he tolerated. It was not possible to count on his father any more. There had to be a man at the head of the house. Samuel was well fitted to fill the place. His brothers obeyed him; to his sisters he was John Chrysostom; he must be very careful. His father wasn't up to much but it is just when one isn't up to much that one wants to be different. He might very well, one day or the other, when she and he were at the town, get hold of the rifle and try to regain the upper hand. She had been thinking about it a lot, that was what had made her so thoughtful these days. She put this with plenty of honey round it. Samuel did not need as much. He took his role seriously.

She made her flight on November 16th. She had said that she was going to Orange. She expected to return that night but not to worry if it was next day. She met a little frozen snow at the approach to the pass at la Nesque. As she knew nothing about driving she was highly pleased with the skidding in the state she was in; it was a dance. She returned that evening. She had seen Clef-des-coeurs. And what was more, he had seen her. The peasant women were not in the habit of watching wrestling, even Greco-Roman. And there was Ennemonde in the front row with lips aglow, eyes shining, and cheeks on fire. And then her size!

She had even executed some business. She wanted to account for everything.

It was at Séderon in the spring that Clef-des-coeurs spoke to her at last. He did more; he invited her to drink a coffee laced with rum, which she did. They sat side by side on the *banquette*. He put his hand on Ennemonde's thigh. There was room for it there. He told his life story: the King of Siam, the White Elephant, the gold medal from the fair at Avignon, the time at Tarascon when he felled the Bull of Vaucluse in one minute; he was timid, he was lonely, he kneaded her thigh. He smelled of violets: his brilliantine. He took Ennemonde into the fields and she got exactly what she had been waiting for.

Clef-des-coeurs was overwhelmed; this was the first heart he had opened. Tenderness struck him all of a heap. Curiously enough (as it may seem) he was called Quadragésime, Joseph. He was a foundling, which is not funny, a child found at Uzès, which is worse, and in 1898, which was worst of all. No proper childhood; nothing so infantile, on the contrary. Until the day when he was big enough to defend himself. Having beaten up his last *patron* (the bursar of the Home) he had five or six days of youthful freedom in the stony hills to the north of Nîmes, then a year on a prison farm. Leaving the lock-up he enlisted voluntarily in the Foreign Legion for seven years. It was at Sidi-Bel-Abbès that he had

himself tattooed with a heart on his chest, on the right
side naturally. The tattooer was an old Englishman who
loved symbols. At the end of his time Quadragésime did
not re-enlist. He was champion of the entire military
district at openhanded wrestling. It was a job. He joined
the outfit of Paul Pons, Au Paradis des Athlètes, at
Marseilles. After that nothing, until Ennemonde. It was
a fact that he was timid and lonely.

Ennemonde made up her mind without delay. The
happiness she had just experienced had been due to her
for a long time and she had every right to it. It was not
a question of continuing to follow the fairs and lying
together behind the bushes. While the sentimental Clef-
des-coeurs walked with her holding her little finger she
was thinking fast. It was then that she thought of the
house of Jules Dupuis, called Bouscarle (whose head
hadn't yet been found). This house, hidden on one of the
darkest mountain-slopes at Pompe was exactly what
they needed while waiting. Waiting for what? That
which was at the back of Ennemonde's mind. The
Dupuis-Melchiors had left the house abandoned, eaten
away daily as it was by the winds, rains and perpetual
shade of the glens. Only a man like Bouscarle could
have lived there, and only a man like the one who held
her little finger would live there from now on, while
waiting. He would remain within call; it would be a
matter of an hour to meet him every night. The Greco-
Roman fell in with everything proposed to him. With
the state of his right heart and his left heart what it
was, he could refuse nothing to this woman who cooed
like a wood-pigeon. The valise that held the carpet, the

White Elephant and the pink trunks was loaded into the B 14.

At the top of the pass Ennemonde hid the car under an oak and led Clef-des-coeurs by short-cuts. It was the first of many nights. They had a great blanket of stars, though there were ghostly animals on the ground. But for his passion the champion of the military district would not have put up with it, especially in those glens, but a hundred and forty kilos of love exert a queer effect on someone who weighs a hundred and ten and has had nothing to chew on till now but heavyweights.

The house in the glens was far from palatial. On the first night they even had to chase out a badger, but, little by little, thanks to the ingenuity of the Greco-Roman and to all the material—sheets, kitchen utensils, stove, and even a table and chairs—brought by Ennemonde, it titivated itself up. It was quite adequate. Besides, as she said amorously, it was only for a time. She was glimpsing the future. She could even see how to bring it about. Clef-des-coeurs had made a vast bed with a litter of beech leaves. That was the chief thing.

They got through the summer with some difficulty; the nights are too short; Ennemonde could only leave her house very late and had to be back before dawn. But she did so regularly without ever failing. But eventually they were rewarded, from the middle of autumn the season was now on their side; every night Ennemonde had to contend with rain and wind and soon she would have to reckon with cold, snow, and the *bise*—fit to tear the horns from an ox—that blows from the Alps and

whose sighings are so romantic as well; but she saw
only the lengthening of the nights.

Therein they found the certainty that their understanding was perfect. Ennemonde in particular needed
this, still having much to do before reaching her goal.
She often contemplated her face in the glass. She found
it beautiful, and with reason; it was. Her eyes did not
have their equals for miles around, even among young
women; the rest of her face was full and luminous,
unmarred by the absence of teeth; on the contrary her
lips, which were rather full, were thereby more sharply
outlined and this definition rendered the faultless purity
of her gaze—which might otherwise have appeared
rather fixed—more human and less divine. Her body?
Ah well, God knows her body was spoiled only by the
bust; clearly her breasts, voluminous but sensitive,
which had nourished thirteen children, were not to
everyone's taste but Clef-des-coeurs was not everyone.
She knew what his hands sought and found when they
caressed her body. Clef-des-coeurs was impressed less by
the shape of this flesh than by its purpose. And as for
this purpose, the rest of the body provided this perfectly.

Often, throughout that winter, in the great bed of
beech leaves that took up all the space in the room,
between the sheets that Ennemonde had chosen as being
the finest in her trousseau (Honoré had never wanted to
use them), under the heavy blankets and sheepskins,
they remained entwined together, motionless.

It was during one of these moments that they heard
someone trying to open the door. No, it was not
Honoré; Honoré, she knew, would go about it in the

biblical manner, she knew this and counted on it. It wasn't the Melchiors either; the Melchiors, strong for their rights, would have broken the door down; so it was someone poking around, someone who did not know that the Melchiors were not responsible for this locking up and bolting. It was in the depth of winter; the person did not persist and they heard him moving off on the crackling snow. It must be someone who was after Bouscarle's million. Ennemonde told the story to Clef-des-coeurs.

People may be happy or unhappy, but the world goes round; after the spring they felt summer coming on. Now Ennemonde had never lost sight of the world. This spring was her limit. One night, as she was leaving the house, she deliberately made a noise when passing by the bakehouse where Honoré slept barricaded. Next day she repeated her stratagem. The door stayed barricaded. She was not surprised, she had foreseen this. One doesn't make thirteen children with a man through a nightdress with a hole in it without knowing how he reacts. She very nearly told Clef-des-coeurs about it but she didn't, she was playing too big a game; it was for her entire future. She did well. On the ninth day, when she returned, she found Honoré standing in the court-yard. At last he was out in the open; he wanted to know where she had been. Two hours later they found him under the mule's hooves.

Ennemonde was a woman of great sense, wise, solid, of enlightened behaviour, equable, integral; and with all this she managed things in exemplary fashion. The eight children that remained to her swore only by her.

They were well-kept, the house shone, her finances prospered. She had never done a sou's worth of damage to anyone. Her size had sheltered her for a long time from feminine jealousies (in which we have seen they erred, but here feminine jealousy was not clearsighted). There was no question, even for a second, of refusing permission for burial. The house in the glen was dismantled, its tenant had disappeared. It remained only to wait a summer. She went twice to Draguignan, once to Séderon. That was all.

In October of the same year Ennemonde received a visit from a front-wheel-drive car that contained a personage who was a fine man by local standards, where no one ever looks at the face; well-dressed, simply but well, for he had a tiepin in the shape of a horseshoe. It was Clef-des-coeurs. He had let his moustache grow and done his hair with the parting in the middle and no kiss-curl, which altered him completely. In addition he carried a *borsalino*.

She enthused noisily in front of her family (and in front of others during the days that followed). It was her cousin Joseph! Didn't they remember up here her cousin Joseph who had gone to Algeria? Ah well, it was he. He seemed to have done well down there. This cousin (distant, she said) was officially recognized by one Martin, of Montbrun, who was Ennemonde's first cousin. He even cited as proof that cousin Joseph had straight away repaid him the money he had borrowed from the family before exiling himself beyond the seas. It must have been a fair sum as Martin sent off an order to Sisteron for a new bus with which he reckoned to start a service

65

in the valley of the Jabron. He never had the time; he was a quarrelsome man, the money made him touchy, and he was killed, before he'd even driven his rattletrap, by a Piedmontese who was arrested at Laragne and tried at Gap. That was clearly taking a risk, but a calculated risk. One can't always do everything oneself; one must also (judiciously) count a little on others.

It was difficult to send cousin Joseph away on these terrible winter nights; for he renewed his visits frequently. He seemed to enjoy the company of the whole family. And he was popular. He told stories of the Arabs and even knew how to do card tricks; finally he presented them with a wireless set. All this in stages. On one side there were Samuel, who was preparing to join his regiment, his brother David, aged eighteen, and the three girls : Judith, Noémie and Rachel, aged seventeen, sixteen and fifteen respectively. These were born during Honoré's grand biblical period. The two following children had died at an early age. These were spoken of vaguely; they were Rodolphe and Andréa. These two had seen the light of day at the beginning of Ennemonde's revolt, when she had attempted to stop thinking in terms of the nightgown with a hole in it and to escape towards romance. Finally, there were the three last surviving children : Ferdinand, Alithéa and Chantal, twelve, eleven and ten years old, born in full flight; Ennemonde's three last pregnancies, exactly counter to her flight, had yielded no fruit of which any memory persisted save for the last, whom she had insisted on calling, quite simply, Paul, which seemed to indicate that even at that moment she was determined to re-enter

66

the century. The most stubborn (but within the bounds of a reasonable opposition) were Judith, Noémie and Rachel. This was normal. Ennemonde was prepared for it. Rachel was the first to yield, having been taken seriously and treated as a young lady for a month at a stretch. Judith and Noémie gave in during a car ride; Rachel's treatment had markedly sensitized them to cousin Joseph's still violet-perfumed attentions.

He had an equal degree of success in the village. It's not known who warned him, perhaps he had a nose for it, but he distinguished very clearly between those whose opinion counted and those one could (and indeed should) take no notice of. Here, then, was an accepted man.

Clef-des-coeurs supposedly lived at Orange or Draguignan or Avignon or Marseilles, it was rather vague, but he came often and made longer and longer stays with a family that was really united from then on, with which he was at ease, and which was at ease with him. One night at table Ennemonde informed him of the purchase of the farm and the pasture and, as if by command, he began to talk of a dream : suppose if, on what had been the yard, they had a new house built, just right, 'with green shutters'. They could have nice 'individual' rooms with painted wallpaper. All this perhaps with central heating, certainly with a bathroom, until he had listed all the delights of Babylon without forgetting the 'ultra-modern' kitchen. The children listened, mouths agape! Ennemonde retorted (as if attracted, but uncertain) that she had no money for such an enterprise. Then on cousin Joseph's part there was a

fine performance of the hand placed on the breast, of
'What I have is yours', 'You are all the family I have!',
and 'I love you as if you were my own kin', ending up
with tears, which were very moving in this face whose
eyes no one had ever seen. For the first time, that evening, there was a general embracing.

Clef-des-coeurs had other embraces, as will be understood, they had been continent only during the critical
period just after Honoré's death and while cousin Joseph
was passing his entrance examination by the family and
the village. As soon as their extreme prudence had
allowed they had hastened to meet fairly regularly in a
wayside shelter over at Apt or, more precisely, at Goult-
Lumière. The bed was small, but it was better than
nothing. Eight months of total abstinence, that had been
too long, but what must be must be and they were nearing their goal.

It was a contractor from Banon who was entrusted
with building the new house. He had some ideas, and an
album, and proposed a kind of Swiss chalet. The chalet
looked good on paper, the whole family was enthus-
iastic. Samuel just had time to see the foundations dug,
then he left for his regiment at Valence. In normal
times the erection of a Swiss chalet at the sheepfold of
le Pendu would have excited curiosity and jealousy.
It happened that this was in '38 and war was threaten-
ing. People talked of it, but very little; they had other
worries.

One day, however, Fouillerot got down from the
lorry that brought the workmen every morning. He said
he had someone to see in those parts but, in fact, he

spent almost the entire day on the site, looking at the dimensions of the building and calculating how much it was going to cost. For Ennemonde it was a shaft of light. She had watched over her love with too much passion to neglect anything at all, and certainly not the tampering with the keyhole at the house in the glen, the night when she had lain still with her beloved. They had taken precautions the next day. They had seen no one but it was a fact, someone had tried to get in. Who? She had passed everyone through her mind. Honoré, no; so-and-so, so-and-so, so-and-so, no; if it was someone who was watching her he would not have tried to get in, it must be someone after the million. She thought of Martin, of Montbrun, but by now he was eating dande-lions by the root. Now she understood : it was Fouillerot. She was more satisfied than frightened.

Fouillerot had two weaknesses : he loved money, and he believed that a former process-server was someone. Before leaving he thought it cunning to make certain allusions that were perfectly well understood. Enne-monde knew that not all game is killed with the same bullet. She had to find the calibre that suited Fouillerot. The former process-server had worked the district, this way and that, for over twenty years; no one put any money away, whatever it might be, without seeking his opinion and even following his advice. In addition to usury he also bought securities and, as he loved a good commission, a large part of these securities were securities with good commissions, so good that they sometimes ended by being securities no longer! True, they still had the outward appearance of being such; they created

enough illusion to be hidden under piles of blankets like
real securities, but in reality they represented shares in
the Trouser-button Mines, or Timbuctoo Tramways.
Here, when anything is stowed away it's for good, and
even if they were put away for as much as a hundred
years the owners of these securities would never perceive
their worthlessness; if they happened to need some ready
money they went to see Fouillerot, who advised them to
sell French government stocks, or Electrical Energy, or
the PLM instead. If they had no French government
stocks or Electrical Energy or PLM, which was rare,
Fouillerot would advise them to hang on to their
Trouser-button Mines and Timbuctoo Tramways,
which were 'due for a rise', which were 'currently in
process of rising', and he would lend the sum they needed
at 7 or 8% a month. To pay the dividends he made
them invest in other securities of the same kind, and
with the money from these investments he paid the
dividends of the preceding investments. This industry
had gone on for over twenty years.

Ennemonde did not understand the mechanism all
at once. To tell the truth, she was far from suspecting all
these ramifications. But, to determine the calibre of the
bullets (or the buckshot) she enquired on this side and
that about Fouillerot. With her commonsense (and her
passion) she soon became aware that she was slowly
bringing to light the springs, the linch-pins and the gear-
wheels that constituted the essence of Fouillerot. And
then she was intrigued by those famous securities. After
all, she had studied for the teachers' training college in
her time! Certainly that did not afford much financial

70

knowledge but she told herself simply : 'French government stocks I know, Electrical Energy I know, PLM I know. This, that and the other I know, but that one I don't know'. Of course she did not know everything and she did not hit on the secret at once; going to the banks at Orange and Carpentras for information, their first reply was : 'Yes, Madame, that's a good security, it is quoted on the Exchange, it's worth so much.' But one fine day they said : 'No, Madame, this security doesn't exist any longer, it's worthless.' Now, my fine fellow !

'Clearly,' she told herself, 'I want the death of this sinner.' She did not become aware of her decision in these precise terms, but it was essential to ward off definitively the danger that might be forthcoming from Fouillerot. For they had found the hoard in the house in the glen. Not the million, the million was in Treasury bonds whose numbers were known and on which a stop had been placed, but something much better than the million : three thousand gold pieces in louis and Swiss federal currency. Which clearly indicated Heaven's intent to protect the lovers' happiness with a firm hand. Soon after the night when someone had fiddled with the lock, and alerted by the subsequent conversation when Ennemonde had mentioned the million, Clef-des-coeurs set himself to undertake a methodical search of the house and to probe its walls; he had learned a few little tricks in the Legion, notably the use of a knitting-needle. He did find it, and on this occasion gave Ennemonde an extraordinary proof of his love. 'This man,' she told herself, trembling in every limb, 'has never had three sous to call his own. Now he

71

has all this gold that he discovered himself this afternoon. He could go away and leave me. We've been
together for three years now and, even supposing he
loved me a little, he might still prefer the gold to me.
He's waited for me and he prefers me to all the gold in
the world.' (She was right; three thousand louis or all
the gold in the world, that's the same in this case.) She
flamed up. An admirable night followed, of which Clef-
des-coeurs did not understand very much, except that he
had never hoped for so much and that Ennemonde was
even better than in their early days. As for her, it was
like being in a forge. It was that night that everything
was decided : the wayward mule, the sharp shaft of
intelligence that banked on the Piedmontese of Sisteron,
the long abstinence of eight months, the play-acting
before the family, and before a family she worshipped;
finally, now, the death of the sinner.

He, Fouillerot, knew of the existence of those three
thousand gold pieces. He had not sold them to Bouscarle,
or not all, but he knew that the man with the dogs
conducted his business in the shoddy offices of the valleys
round about and there existed a sort of jungle tom-tom
between his colleagues and himself. They did not say
everything but they did say certain things; the rest could
be guessed. When he had gone to talk about the
Treasury bonds and to advise that a stop be placed on
them, it was to keep a finger in the pie. He had even,
soon afterwards, made an oblique proposition in his own
peculiar style to the Dupuis-Melchiors. 'If, by chance,
you should find the bonds,' he told them, 'don't tell
anyone, come to see me. It's not worth having the State

poking its nose into this affair, you'll be left with nothing. Don't you worry about the stop, I'll see to that myself.' He proposed, in the event, and taking the stop into account, to give them 10% of the parcel; it was a tentative hope, but one never knew, so he kept his options open with regard to the Melchiors. To leave nothing to chance he went more than twenty times, at night, to explore the house in the glen. The twenty-first time he found the door closed. For a moment he thought it might be the work of the Melchiors, but the Melchiors were stupid creatures, it was impossible to credit them with the vestige of an idea, even so simple a one as that of locking the door. He kept watch. Finally he heard movement within, and voices. He kept guard until the morning. He saw Ennemonde leave. Ah, my fine friend !

Since Honoré's death Ennemonde's looks had improved. Happiness suited her. Her grossness had firmed up. Her hair was still like pitch, her skin clear, fine and soft, transparent with a blush of bright blood. She used a very small spot of rouge at the middle of her lips, rice powder scented with almond. And her eyes ! Oh, what purity ! Nothing was purer than those eyes, whose lashes, an inch long, darkened the circuit of her gaze ! She went to see Fouillerot alone (no point in exposing Clef-des-coeurs too much). The former process-server, despite having been marinated in stamped paper for fifty years, was disconcerted by the purity of those eyes; not touched, of course, not moved or softened or anything of that kind, but disconcerted, so much so that he did not immediately understand the terms of the letter

73

Ennemonde had just handed him. He was firmly convinced that she would surrender unconditionally, incited to think so by her wearing her best clothes. What was the meaning of this letter-head of the Crédit Lyonnais? He looked up; he saw another look. Then he began to read attentively. It was clear and simple. This letter, signed by the Director of a great bank, declared that the Trouser-button Mines, the Tramways of Timbuctoo, the Casino of Trifoullis-les-oies, the Wire and Rolling Mills of Hoggar, Cuzco Rubber, the Badabada-Oudououdou Railway and other similar Russian loans were not worth a rabbit's fart, reeked only of fraud. It was only necessary to spread this information. . . . He tried to fight. 'They'll be worried about their losses and the trick you've played them,' said Ennemonde. 'They won't care a damn about what I get and the trick I've played you. Who'll believe you? Who'll believe a thief?' Fouillerot had a son who was studying for a law degree at Aix-en-Provence. Thief? No, it would be intolerable! And yet, there was the letter from the Crédit Lyonnais, and he was better placed than anyone to know that it told the truth. He gave in. He thought he was done with it; he was wrong. Ennemonde did not intend to run the slightest risk.

The Swiss chalet was a mistake, she knew that. The first, the sole error; it would have to be paid for none the less. But God wanted Ennemonde to be happy and the war broke out. They moved into the new house just when Hitler was bellowing. Ennemonde thought about Fouillerot, until the defeat; it was a difficult time to endure anyway—the whole family in the same boat and impossible to make love freely because of the children.

After the proclamation of the defeat things went smoothly. Samuel was a prisoner; Ennemonde and Clef-des-coeurs went off to get married without any fuss at Avignon. Everyone understood that, there had to be a man in the house. This marriage for love, that no one would have pardoned, passed for a marriage of convenience. After the Occupation, David joined the *maquis*. It was easy, one had only to leave the house. Several resistance members of this kind, that is, all the young people of the district old enough to be sent to Germany, installed themselves in the shepherds' huts in the wilder parts and in the glens. Clef-des-coeurs victualled them regularly. It wasn't a matter of taking up a stand, it was natural. As soon as he saw rifles and machine-guns in the hands of these young people he felt a gust of nostalgia, the Legion tickled his shoulderblades. There was no shadow of calculation in all this. It was the slope that God himself places before the feet of his friends. Ennemonde was making money. She was engaged in a very good black market. They had set up a clandestine butchery in the old premises. There was really nothing secretive about it; as she provisioned not only the *maquis* of the huts and the glens but those of Séderon and La Bohémienne, the *gendarmes* knew when to close their eyes. It was not for lack of receiving anonymous denunciations. The hand of Fouillerot could be recognized in some. One morning he was found dead in front of his door. He had been shot at close quarters and with a very sensitive weapon. He was owed plenty of money to right and left. The son had the good sense to remain at Aix.

Ennemonde's story was coming to an end; there was nothing more in store for her after Fouillerot's death, unless it was what ordinary mortals call success. Having had to mount guard over her happiness, Ennemonde had learnt many things about the life of feeling, and notably that pure gold always ends up by changing into base lead. Already she no longer had that devouring hunger; she knew that Clef-des-coeurs was in the same state. True, what remained would have feathered the nests of twenty couples but, taking everything into account, when one thought of the sacrifices it had taken to raise the four walls of this conjugal chamber, one wondered if the game had been worth the candle. It wasn't a question of heart, of the heart on one side and life on the other. She still loved; often she still walked on air. But she had as much joy, and exercise, in making money. She was making as much as you care to think of. She supplied the entire valley with black-market meat and with tacit approval, for she completely revictualled the rebels of the glens and the surrounding rocky massifs. The clandestine butchery at le Pendu functioned day and night. Ennemonde was obliged to travel alone to conduct romantic negotiations at Orange, Avignon, Carpentras; once she even went as far afield as Grenoble and Marseilles. She had to knock on secret doors at night, encounter hangdog looks, make herself respected. She had to buy people, 'decent' men, strong men, who became humble and submissive when she showed the money. Every time this happened she felt that glowing sensation and that delightful hammering on the anvil that had bound her to Clef-des-coeurs. She would have found it difficult to dispense with these new emotions; sometimes she preferred them to those of the marriage chamber. She understood also that she had utterly enjoyed Honoré and Martin, and even Fouillerot, while sacrificing them.

'Cousin Joseph' bought the flocks and managed the slaughtering. Every Wednesday he went off with the van to provision the *maquis*. They were on velvet, the Germans were not only far away but their routes by-passed the area. They didn't even see the tail of one. Clef-des-coeurs also spent some very romantic nights in the open. He loved being with these groups of young people; he talked to them of his time in the Foreign Legion. Towards the end of the Occupation the high mountain wastes were used for parachute drops of arms. Clef-des-coeurs was delighted to lend a hand in the collection and distribution of this manna from heaven. He met the delegates of the neighbouring *maquis*, with whom he didn't get on very well. They demanded the lion's share. He wanted to keep a heavy machine-gun. (It came from the depot at Orange.) Finally he had his way. He initiated David into the handling of the weapon. He dreamed of it at night. When he was at the Swiss chalet he fretted over the magnificent weapon. Have they greased it as I told them? Have they put on its jacket? Whenever he had a free moment he went off to look at it and fiddle with it. One night, lying beside Ennemonde, he thought of Abd-el-Krim; not for long, a flash, but it was the first time since the end of his seven years' service; and yet, before Ennemonde, he had been entirely alone.

The parachute drops were betrayed. Seven truckloads of S.S. with police dogs climbed up to the wastelands by way of Banon. They had not even broached the hairpin-bends of Redortiers when Clef-des-coeurs, alerted by public rumour, rushed off by short-cuts to the glens. Ennemonde was at Avignon that day. He found the camp in a ferment. There were a dozen children of twenty there. He showed them how they could dominate the glens by giving ground over which the enemy would be unable to advance; the slopes on this north side, towards the valley of the Jabron, were very steep, thickly covered with great box-trees, juniper and white oak, and interspersed with bluffs; they had only to crawl in there, and take good care not to try to cross the valley but to stay in the nearby foot-hills, and it would take Alexander's army to dislodge them. 'As for me,' he said, 'I'm going to make a bit of a noise while you hop it.' And he got them to give him the heavy machine-gun with five boxes of belts. David insisted on staying with him; he found it perfectly normal, he had learnt the job of mate. David and he had time to dig a hole in a magnificent position. From above they commanded the three slopes that climbed up to them; the fourth, inaccessible, side was buttressed against the northern precipice.

It took the air-force to finish them off. Clef-des-coeurs had never had such a marvellous time. The machine-gun popped away (he had always wanted to own a motorcycle); while he slaughtered the S.S. and their dogs he was happy to think of Ennemonde's presence in the background. He never loved anyone as he loved David. Towards the evening of the second day a hedge-hopping aeroplane machine-gunned them, but it had to return five times.

Ennemonde wept for months, peacefully. She was possessed by a great calm.

She was woken up after the Liberation. She was the wife and mother of two heroes. The Prefect came to attention and gave her a military salute. She attended banquets, in the place of honour; she presided at others. A county councillor who was a dentist suggested that he should make her a denture. For nothing. She accepted. She went to him several times for the impressions. He was a redhaired man dressed in white. Which is always delightful. But while he was leaning over her mouth she felt his weight and found him too light. 'No,' she told herself, 'it's over.' Since it was over she allowed herself to weigh up everyone around her. Often, at these Liberation banquets which were repeated almost every week, she calculated the weight of certain guests, allowing herself to be drawn into reverie by big moustaches, big cheeks, big necks, without ever feeling the slightest glow. 'No,' she told herself, 'it's all over.' Besides, she thought unceasingly of Clef-des-coeurs, of Cousin Joseph, of M. Quadragésime (whose name she now bore). She had known him in all his aspects, and in all his aspects he had filled her to overflowing. Every time she was astonished to feel happy at his death; then this astonishment ceased when she understood that it was not happiness but peace, and that it was not a matter of death but of separation from the object of her passion. She had been aware of the necessity for this rupture, but she would never have had the courage to envisage it coolly and to take it to its logical conclusion as she had with Honoré. It was foretold that she would never handle lead, always gold.

She received her denture by post and, despite the first well-meaning intentions of the county councillor, a bill, which she paid. Samuel, returned from captivity, busied himself with the le Pendu sheepfold and the flocks. Judith and Noémie were married; the first to the oldest son of the Café des Boulomanes, at Carpentras, a soft-drink affair that went off very well; Noémie had married a tax inspector who had been a member of the *maquis* group protected by the 'sacrifice' of Clef-des-coeurs and David. This inspector was in a fair way to gaining rapid promotion, but he had had to accept a post in the Aisne. The family wrote regularly. Rachel kept constant company with Siméon Richard, of Saumane, the one who had killed 'the horrible thing' and who had been nicknamed ever since Siméon Chien-loup. They made a nice couple but they could not make up their minds one way or the other and, as they did nothing to compromise themselves during the summer, it was necessary to await their good pleasure. They refused any other match, they were always together, and nothing seemed to come of it. Ferdinand had been spoiled by the Occupation period. In 1941 he had been sent to the lycée at Avignon as a boarder. He could have shone there; he stuck at an honest average. He failed his baccalauréat, refused to sit again, and stayed at the farm where Samuel welcomed him with demonstrations of unparalleled joy. He had been very upset by David's death. After his return Ennemonde had urged him to get married; he had refused with more energy than is usual on such occasions, an energy resembling anger. Yet he did not seem to be happy on his own. Ferdinand's arrival transformed him. It was a kind of love. 'Good, good,' Ennemonde told herself, 'those boys take after me'. In her view things would stay like that for them for a good part of their lives; but for them, too, would come the moment of the 'base lead'; only she would no longer be there, and perhaps the moment might not ever come. The girls took after Honoré. Especially Alithéa, who was a mathematical genius. She was as pretty as a picture but her intelligence was quite independent of her body, and it was clear as day that she was interested only in intelligence. Her teacher had written to Ennemonde; it was he who had spoken of genius. 'In my whole career,' he said, 'I have never been confronted with such obvious genius.' He gave advice as to the course Alithéa should follow henceforward and spoke of what she should do after the degrees and examinations (in the plural) which he regarded as unimportant formalities. Alithéa was sent to the Polytechnique at Grenoble. As for Chantal, she resolved the problem that had remained unsettled since 1913, she entered the teachers' training college at Digne.

The denture made Ennemonde ugly. She tried it, looked at herself in the glass, and removed the appliance; she had never seen such an ogreish face! A little later she noticed that her looks were going. Despite the excellence of her mirror, the one in which, time and again, she had found herself beautiful, she saw herself distorted, as if reflected in water. It was old age into which, little

81

by little, she was advancing. Her size, without increasing, became enormity; her weight burdened her, she suffered pains and, at the same time, remorse, which increased proportionately as she lost the power of movement. Her children had never ceased to worship her, they waited on her hand and foot, especially Samuel and Ferdinand, who looked after the farm, and Rachel, still a spinster, who was responsible for the housework. Chantal had a job as a schoolteacher in the district. She had bought a *deux-chevaux* and came to see her mother. Alithéa was in Paris, but she wrote every week with astonishing regularity. Her colleagues at the Institute of Scientific Research would have been amazed at the tone of these letters. This girl, against whom all the examinations, contests and certificates in the world were crushed like snowflakes against the windscreen of a car, without slowing its advance in the slightest, had only one love : her mother. Even love is too small a word to depict the feeling that she expressed in four pages of almost childish writing every Wednesday that God made; it was the distracted admiration of a pupil for a beloved master, an endless stammering of admiration. Yet Alithéa was regarded by her peers as sure of a future Nobel Prize and Ennemonde had failed her entrance examination to the teachers' training college. Noémie and her tax inspector (posted to the Manche) wrote equally regularly. Only the café proprietress at Carpentras, Judith, remained somewhat distant. This was, first, because she had become very rich, but mainly because she had devoted the back room of her café (where there used to be two billiard-tables) to exhibitions of paintings. Her two children, registered at birth as Pierre and Jeanne, she now called Patrick and Ghislaine.

The pains continued to increase and diversify. Confined now to her armchair, Ennemonde listened to the past as one listens to the murmuring of the sea in a shell. She saw herself in action. She marvelled and trembled at her past. 'It's not possible,' she told herself, 'you couldn't have done such a thing. How could you do such a thing? It isn't you, it wasn't you; you've made it up.' Then, when all this past became clear in deed and detail, she said to herself : 'No, it really is you. You. You did everything that seems so extraordinary, but in order to succeed you had to lend a hand in so many even more extraordinary and dangerous things.' She frightened herself, she shivered. She was ravished. She wept in very moving fashion, without ridiculous fuss, just as in the great tragedies; great tears filled her eyes and the famous 'rivulets' beloved of the romantics trickled down her cheeks. Her children gathered round her and consoled her. At first, these misunderstandings delighted her, eventually she no longer realized that there were any misunderstandings and merely felt very lucky to have such attentive children.

She kept Alithéa's letters in the pocket of her apron. When she had ten of them she asked for a piece of string to tie them up and Rachel put the bundle in a drawer of the commode; there were several hundred letters already and a stranger who read them one after the other would have been thunderstruck by these inexhaustible and desperately monotonous litanies of adoration. Now, at twenty-five, Alithéa had published *An Essay on*

83

Perfect Axiomatization in the Study of Invariables and Lattice Theory that made her sought after by every scientific centre in the world. She had made three visits to the USSR and two to the USA; she had long been regarded as a scholar with the greatest possible future and she was working on *Some Doubts as to the Identity of Chemical Properties in Isotopic Elements.*

One Friday, the day the post came, having read one of these famous letters, so like all the others, Ennemonde said : 'Send for Alithéa.' They sent a telegram. Alithéa arrived at Marignane on the Sunday, hired a car, and reached the Swiss chalet on the Tuesday morning. She was still as pretty as ever. It was nearly winter and Ennemonde's armchair had been moved near the stove. Alithéa kissed her mother and caressed for a long time the thick white hair that Rachel had arranged in two bandeaus separated by a parting; they spoke of this and that. Ennemonde and Alithéa were alone for only a moment in the day, when Rachel went down to the cellar to fetch some logs.

'The night your father died,' said Ennemonde, 'were you awake?'

'No,' answered Alithéa.

'Did you hear or see anything?'

'No,' answered Alithéa.

These Nos meant Yes.

Alithéa stopped writing. Soon afterwards she married an elderly professor.

Life at the Swiss chalet was simple. It would be a complete mistake to think of Samuel and Ferdinand as having the guise and demeanour of the classical peasant, or even Rachel. They were not cultivators but shepherds. The money their mother had made during the war guaranteed them complete independence and it is very good for the soul to have a skeleton in the cupboard. Moreover, a monument had been raised on the little fort where the two heroes had 'sacrificed' themselves and Ennemonde had been decorated. The two brothers and Rachel lived in perfect harmony. Samuel concerned himself with the buying and selling, Ferdinand with the shepherds; he visited the pastures every day in his jeep; Rachel kept house and looked after their mother. As she was still a mother of a hundred and thirty kilos, and very soft kilos by now, the brothers relieved her when they were there; and when they were not there Siméon Chien-loup lent a hand in settling Ennemonde into her armchair or helping her with her requirements. These four persons—Samuel, Ferdinand, Rachel and Siméon—never raised their voices; it was as if the house were empty, the work seemed to get done by the operation of the Holy Spirit.

After Alithéa's marriage Ennemonde began to take an interest in the outside world. She had two of the windows of the Swiss chalet enlarged, at the east and west, and she had a smaller one made at the north and one at the south; she did not count the glass door that opened on the south-east terrace. They bought a wheelchair. She had regained a little strength in her wrists and finally managed to move herself unaided from one window to another during the bad weather; in summer she even crossed the threshold and went out on the terrace. She regarded the world with an easy conscience.

The sky is transparent. The air intoxicating. The wind sounds in the pines like the sea. The grass bends, the lavender quivers. Tiles clatter as if someone were walking on the roof. The wind echoes in the depths of the cisterns. The paths smoke, the beeches stir, the birches sway, the poplars glint, the wind runs in the grass like a fox. The arch of the walls whistles. The latches dance in their fastenings. The shutters, fastened, bang on their hooks; a stable-door groans. Straw flies. The wind blows masses of starlings like a flood of marble blocks. A rook drowns in mid air, crying out. Now it is far away. It can no longer be heard. It disappears. The wind has no substance and yet it obscures the afternoon light. All the noises from up-wind come in a jumble. Down there in the north, ten or twenty kilometres from the far side of the valley of the Jabron, there are flocks moving on the mountain of Saint-Clerc; pine-forests which moan around the roc de la Gloriette; tractors ploughing up the lavender fields on the flanks of Chanleduc; lorries labouring at the hairpin bends of the gorges of the Méouge; muleteers moving towards the eagle's rock with belled collars, who are not local but probably from the valley of Barcelonnette; the distant horn of the rail-car from Marseilles to Grenoble borne on the wind just as the leading coach reaches the level-crossing at La Clapine (so it must be four o'clock—or sixteen hours if you prefer it); the rail-car can be heard only when it reaches this exact spot and only along the axis of Sisteron-Laragne because, fifty metres from the level-crossing, it emerges, snout in air, on the plateau at the end of an ascent and the wind snatches its bellow as it comes and carries it over the five mountains—l'Adret, Saint-Cirq, Rongnouse, Saint-Martin, Pelegrine—to spill it finally over the High Country; it takes a good ear to distinguish it, or long practice; then one knows it's four o'clock or sixteen hundred hours if you like, it's of absolutely no importance for whoever is long used to it thinks as little of the time as of his first slipper! There are carts in the Jabron valley, but one must be very circumspect to become aware of this. The sound is not heard as it is, the valley is too narrow; to catch it down there the wind must plunge from the height of Saint-Clerc, picking up on the mountainside all that's happening at Curel, where they sound the bells over every meadow, at Bevons, where a demolition firm is constructing new terraces with bulldozers, at Miravail where, nine times out of ten in all weathers, except the white of winter, the flocks are gathered to be counted. Thus what one hears of the carts in the valley must be subject to caution. The more so as, in rising from the Jabron, and already burdened with all the above, the wind swoops and carries away all the sounds of the glens, and especially those extraordinary ones made by the box-trees, the june-berries, the white oaks and the waterfalls, without reckoning that a motorcycle climbing the Négron is enough to falsify the indications altogether. Anyone who can tell whether a car, or two, or the bus are going from Omergues to Noyers or vice versa is pretty sharp. Some can. Ennemonde can, she is even able to tell the make of car, and hence the name of its owner. When the little schoolteacher at Saint-Vincent changed her *deux-chevaux* for a Renault, Ennemonde knew it two days later. Ennemonde and the shepherds who inhabit these parts, and the wanderers who exist in the High Country: woodcutters, charcoal-makers, or romantic gadabouts, sentimental itinerants, individuals with fuck-all to do, who stroll from north to south, from east to west and along every diagonal, eating a crust here, sipping a cup of coffee there, warming their hands in front of a stove in one place and sleeping in the hay or stable-litter in another, or simply in the black cold—these too are equally skilled at telling the true from the false. They go even further, they really make it their job and in ninety-nine per cent of cases they make a living of it. Not only can they sense the direction of the smallest pattering borne on the wind—that's the children coming out of school at Séderon, that's the motor-scooter of the chap who runs the postal service at Barret, that's the pulley of César Durand's barn at Ferrassière—but they can distinguish smells. No matter if it travels over thousands of hectares of lavender in flower, over hay, over pink clover, cess-pits, townships without drains, over building-site latrines or a thousand carburettors, it's enough for someone to grill a cutlet in some corner for these wanderers to bend their course towards the blessed spot from which the odour emanates. Much more so when it has to do with the religious mumbo-jumbo that follows the cutting of a pig's throat. Especially as they always choose a week with a settled, dry wind, rather cool, lightly perfumed with the first rosemary flowers, and a sky of polished blue without the least trace of haze. When all these conditions co-exist the wanderer, the itinerant, the fine sinister fellow who travels over plains, peaks, valleys and plateaux is at once on the alert. He walks against the wind so as to breathe in every detail. He has previously taken the precaution to get as far south as possible, so as to get to leeward of the greatest possible number of farms, hamlets and villages. Starting from there he reascends, tacking to and fro.

Nearly always, now that the peasantry is, ostensibly, industrialized, the slaughterer, an aristocratic type, is one of these very itinerants. When the animal reaches the desired weight a courier is dispatched abroad to search out so-and-so, called such-and-such; once found, the latter considers the weather, tests the wind, looks at the moon and appoints a day. Naturally, his colleagues know him for what he is. Without ever having rubbed shoulders with him, a thing these recluses never do, for they always keep several kilometres apart from each other, they know that so-and-so, called such-and-such, journeys with a case of knives; at times they've even heard him sharpening his knives on a flint, a characteristic sound borne by the wind whose significance can escape no one whose only concern is the search for food. Anyone who normally feeds on snails, sometimes raw, and small game, sometimes cooked, is immediately interested in the sound of knives being sharpened. He knows that it's pointless to try to follow so-and-so, called such-and-such, that this is the best way of losing him. So he goes down south as far as possible and reascends, beating up against the wind.

The slaughterer goes about his business taking a thousand precautions (and only God knows if God is the solitary's inspiration); going into farms which are not

89

the one he seeks, he leaves by the back door, and sometimes he even starts out a day or two before his appoint-
ment so as to have time to arrange his bag of tricks.
That's why it's useless to follow him. These folk who
wander over the plateau, fireless and homeless, are
drawn from every class of society, from every category.
There are *bourgeois* on the loose, bankrupts, disconso-
late widowers, disinherited younger sons, the lazy, many
lazy ones, petty criminals who have offended against
petty justice, anarchists, idealists, the timorous, simple-
minded or frankly mad. They do no one any harm. They
steal nothing, even those who were used to steal in
the Low Country. They wander about; they are rarely
encountered, and when one does meet one there is a
momentary qualm, because of his appearance and his
silence, but it passes. In the heart of winter they are
severally welcomed in the farms (even the lunatics)
where they render minor services. Some of them, a sort
of kings or emperors, never take shelter with a house-
holder, whatever the weather. Where do they go on
those terrible winter nights? That's their secret! There
they go, scattered over more than a hundred square kilometres, the little gods who snuff the wind, seeking the
smell of fat.

The slaughterer installs himself in the farm courtyard.
The sacrificial animal is brought in despite its cries;
a strange thing, it's enough for the slaughterer to rub
his knives together to silence the animal at once. When
he's a good slaughterer. But he is usually a good slaughterer if he has been chosen from among the wanderers.
Some farmers send for professional butchers. Professional

butchers are not good slaughterers. The animals do not accept the death they bring; if the butcher arrives at the farm, even on a friendly visit, the pigsty, the sheepfold, even the stable, are in turmoil. The wanderer arrives with his knives; all remains calm; there is just a little groaning when the great moment approaches. If one enquires about the basis for this strange behaviour, it is apparent that it is a matter of ceremonial, pure and simple; whether one is destined for sausages or for resurrection, death is the very moment when nature returns at the gallop. Now with the butcher, it's just technique, all he cares about is the relation between the weight of flesh and the weight of money. The wanderer comes from the depths of the ages, he lives arm-in-arm with hunger; one can rely on his respecting the rites; and, in fact, everything goes off with enviable rapidity, ease and civility. The animal is already bleeding into the bucket, like a cask whose bung has been opened, in the simplest way in the world.

Afterwards the body is washed with boiling water, scraped, rubbed, depilated, combed, pumice-stoned, then hung up by the hindlegs to be disembowelled. The smell of this open belly parts at random on the breeze. It is a very pathetic smell. It is that which is exhaled by a battlefield, on the first day. It functions there in the opposite sense to martial music. At the same time, in these immensities that the mountains exalt to the sky, the smell of this animal interior, these surprised viscera, cut short in the middle of their chemical activity, allows the recluses to check the account they draw up every day. It gives rise to an irresistible appetite, a frantic need to feed the machine.

The fat is melted in a large cauldron. The odour produced by this operation is full of information. The kind of wood that is burned indicates the name of the farm, or at least its situation; ordinary beech-wood may have a hundred different scents according as to whether it is dry, damp, covered with lichen from the far north, or riddled by the cantharides worm, according as to whether it is cut into sticks or blocks, according as to whether it has been cut at full moon or new moon, and so on to extra fine subtleties such as, for instance, whether it has been stored in woodsheds, in the open air or shut up in a bakehouse, and especially if it comes from a woodshed constructed according to the rules of the art or knocked up in slapdash fashion. All is at once made known by the scent.

These are merely preliminary indications, but suffice for the wanderer who receives them to bend his course towards the north, the east or the west (the south does not count, it is the side where the wind disappears).

Ennemonde goes even further in interpreting these signs; she is as acute as the itinerants to grasp the significance of the finest gradations. She knows as well as they do the habits and compulsions imposed on every individual; that, for example, at the Valigranes, called Waterloo (no one knows why) the wood is always damp; that at the Martins, called Perussons (this is a small wild pear), it is always dry, even too dry; that at the Graniers, called Marion (it was one of their aunts who was flighty) the woodsheds are marvels of architecture and marquetry, while at the Curbans, known as Monkey's

Arse (because they have a flattened nose), they stack the wood any old way. But she deciphers many more things in the wind. When the fat begins to melt, Ennemonde can give the name and Christian name of the man, or more often the woman, who is stirring the cauldron with the skimmer. There is a flavour of caramel that comes from not taking the trouble to stir the residues into the melting fat, and this is the particular way of doing it of Dorothée Dupuis of the Dupuis-Brouettes (as distinct from the Dupuis-Automobile); if, on the other hand, there arrives a slight perfume of violets, this is pure clean fat, white as snow, whose confection has been entrusted to a master, and that can only be at the Martels, called Charles (a souvenir of the primary school), and because it's little Alexandre who watches over the cauldron, a lad of twelve but already fully informed on everything that is involved in running a *ménage*. *Ménage* here means *domaine* in the sense given to that word between Clovis and Charlemagne—a vast organization of rural craftsmen—and still used in that sense in the High and even in the Low Country. Before modern times had brought about the installation there of an atomic establishment an example that used to be cited was the '*ménage* of Cadarache'.

When the fat is all melted and has been poured off into jars, there remains at the bottom of the cauldron a golden gritty crackling residue known as the *grignons*. It is these residues that are claimed by the wanderers, and their claim must be justified since it is recognized. The *grignons* are strained in a sieve, a screw of paper is filled with them, and this screw of paper is given to the first of the itinerants who shows his head above the wall of the courtyard. The latecomers, they are sometimes two or three, never more, have to content themselves with a little of the fry-up or a few inches of black pudding.

Ennemonde is one of these wanderers, despite her total paralysis, and perhaps just by virtue of this paralysis. She has not, of course, entirely forgotten her actions though she tries to forget them, not that she regrets anything in particular; on the contrary, she is very proud of what she has done and would do it again if necessary, but she wants to forget from a kind of humility. It seems to her that, having succeeded so perfectly, it is important for her to be delivered from all pride and that she should render to God what belongs to God. For without Him she might have been caught redhanded at least three times. That is why she refuses to turn in on herself and why she observes the world. Thanks to the intelligence of her observation she is a part of it; she is swallowed up in it and disappears in it. This is the habitual resource of sinners (or of those whom everyday morality labels sinners); the more 'mortal' the sin, the more substance there is in the world and the more spirit it provides with this substance.

This is so true that, at certain moments, when she has properly cast her accounts, Ennemonde sends Rachel to fetch a paper of *grignons*; as if she needed them! She, who has everything here if she wishes (and she does wish), stuffed plovers simmered in the earthenware casserole, trout that Ferdinand goes to fish for her in the Jabron, *boeuf en daube* a hundred times better than

94

that she used to eat at the table d'hôte (but which she doesn't find any better, even though it is stewed for a long time with pork-rind); she who has more than twenty pigs in her sties a good deal fatter than the one whose throat has been cut today at Joseph Négrel's, called the Zulu, where the smell has been coming from. And Rachel is not ashamed. Rachel understands that Ennemonde is entitled to the *grignons*. And Joseph Négrel may be well aware that Ennemonde has twenty pigs in her sties but he will give Rachel the paper of *grignons* (if she is the first to arrive) because he is well aware that Ennemonde has a claim to them. Of course, he doesn't know about the past, no one knows, but he acts on the assumption that, without well-established rights, people like Ennemonde would not come to ask for the *grignons*.

Like an old queen, she is very content that she should be paid homage, if only because of her good looks and because she has seen through to the hearts of men and women, and because, since she has been immobilized, she has learned to understand the winds, the rains, the storms and the sun. And she is to be seen just like a queen, up there on the terrace of the Swiss chalet, seated in her armchair (on her throne, as she says, for it is a chair with a hole in it), muffled in rugs and shawls or covered with her large straw sombrero, according to the season, smoking her *Voltigeur* (for that has become her addiction), keeping an exact record of every passer-by, calling them by their names, their Christian names, their surnames, or studying them silently, puffing clouds of cigar smoke towards them; gossiping, asking someone to do her a small service such as to go to pick three daisies in the meadow or ten violets on the far slope behind the beech, services that she does not need—Rachel goes to find daisies and violets for her when she really wants them—but services that she asks those close to her whom she loves, with the sole object of giving them a good conscience.

From the month of May on she is installed, or installs herself, slowly turning the wheels of her chair with her swollen hands, on the chalet terrace facing east. This orientation is not usual, she is only sheltered from the wind when facing south, but she chooses the east, first because this is the side from which the spring comes, and also because she wants to enjoy the cold north light that she loves and which strikes her obliquely. One might think that the month of May is rather early to put a paralysed woman out on a terrace where the first warmth of spring does not arrive until the 14th of July. But Ennemonde is sheathed in fat, she is a whale who could tolerate the ice of the North Pole. Moreover, she has herself wrapped up in a shepherd's cloak with three collars and a hood and she has a charcoal footwarmer under her feet.

She has just spent the entire winter beside the kitchen stove. True, the windows of the Swiss chalet are large and well-sheltered, she can contemplate a hundred kilometres of snow or a hundred kilometres of noonday darkness pounded by the wind. But it is just the fact of being under cover that spoils her enjoyment. It's abundantly clear that she has the family problems to chew over, but it's not enough, or it's an aliment that does not satisfy her hunger. There have been no more letters from

Alithéa since her marriage. As for that one, Ennemonde has long watched with interest the victorious struggle she wages against mathematics; to some extent this is closely allied to the struggle one must wage against life if one wants to survive. Nowadays the only news there is of Alithéa comes via the radio, the television, or the newspapers of the extreme Left, which crack her up and publish her photograph every time she discovers that two and two don't make four. What does she intend to do with this left wing? It's her husband who has driven her to it; incapable of giving her a child, he gives her ideas. It's a pity she's so pretty! She really needed to burden herself with a husband! Her figures were daily bread enough for her. One might understand if she sacrificed her beauty to find happiness in numbers, the falsity of which can be unmasked only with extreme cleverness; but to sacrifice her fine youth to, 'Move over there and make room for me', is to waste time playing Puss-in-the-corner, and that isn't very thrilling to watch. The café-owner's wife at Carpentras is almost better-off. Now there's someone who has her work cut out for her with her desire for the romantic. She has no sooner departed for the enchanted forests than the telephone rings: it is her banker, who informs her of a formidable profit on her recently-bought shares, of a distribution of free shares, the lot! She has to come back. Her Patrick and Ghislaine are smug blockheads whose adenoids have been removed in vain. Her husband is grossly over-weight, he is bursting his skin, something that never happened to Ennemonde who is three times as big as he is, but whose skin has always supply adjusted itself.

97

Yes, it's much more interesting to wonder how the café-owner's wife will manage to convert her capital gains into happiness. While here, outside the Swiss chalet, winter rages with its coal-black sky, its snow dark as far as eye can reach, its brutal wind. There remains Rachel. Every evening Siméon Chien-loup comes to see his loved one. This comedy has gone on for ten years now. Whatever the weather, the door opens at the appointed time, the wind rushes in and deposits Siméon Chien-loup in the kitchen of the Swiss chalet. Squalls, storms, tempests, cyclones, blow you horns of Hell! He doesn't care a fuck, he arrives. A curious thing, he arrives on foot. Yet he has three cars, two of them ancient, but three cars none the less, counting the jeep he uses to revictual his shepherds, the Ford which dates back to the year dot but which is still a good goer, and a brand-new Peugeot. Granted that he doesn't want to dirty his Peugeot (the roads are bad), but the Ford? Or at least the jeep? It's a good dozen kilometres from Siméon's to the Swiss chalet. Ennemonde has suspected that there was something at the bottom of all this that was worth discovering. For two or three winters she has patiently arranged it so that she should be alone with Siméon Chien-loup for a moment and little by little, with this word and that, she has wormed his secret out of him. And she was staggered by it! One should never despair of one's children; consider Rachel here, it can't be said that she's very goodlooking, yet do you know why Siméon Chien-loup comes on foot? Why he faces the wind over twelve kilometres of difficult roads on this plateau where winter rages? It's because if he came by car it would be too short. It would be too easy, he wouldn't have the feeling of coming to see the one he loves; whereas, in doing his twelve kilometres every night in the icy darkness, he can't forget that he's going toward something precious, he has the time to be fully aware of it and to savour it. And he has savoured it for ten years! How is Siméon Chien-loup going to end up? And Rachel, how will she end up? These are interesting questions to put to oneself while the winter rages outside (sometimes in total calm), a problem worth attempting to resolve while the snow falls and the darkness round the flakes is clearly visible. There is not just one solution, there are a thousand. She can see them all. She licks her chops over them, but the winter is long.

And there comes a moment when she needs not just to picture violence but to see it in action. Then she puts her swollen hands on the wheels of her chair and, mobilizing all her energy, wheels herself as far as the terrace, facing east. It is from there that the spring comes. It's not a matter of the poets' spring. And indeed, it's not too clear what Ennemonde can want, nowadays, with flower-enamelled meadows and birdsong and other nonsense. It's a real spring that she needs. And that she gets.

It is heralded by an inky blackness that fills up every breach in the Alps. This is not cloud, it is the colour of the sky wounded by the wind. For the moment it is still engaged in stripping the poplars of Piedmont. It comes from Dalmatia, the Adriatic has iced it, the sands of Ravenna have reddened it. It rages against the Alps. Turin crackles with the sparks shot off from the clashing wires of its tramways.

The Dalmatian wind bursts into the valley of Suze and of Exiles, it is at Oulz, it is at Cézane, it bridles against Mount Tabor, l'Aigle Rouge, le Chaberton, the slopes of le Gondron, it claws bellowing against the ridges of le Pelvoux, it flattens the fir plantations of le Lauzet and the larch forests of Orcières, it scourges the meadows of the Viso; it engulfs ice, snow, avalanches in the strange wastes baptized in its annual raging : Archinard, Estario, Pusterle, Viandre, and emerges at last above Chorges.

At this moment, in the Swiss chalet, Ennemonde has seen the sky darken nearer and nearer, coming towards her. Already there is a small something of great interest to her in the far depth of the zenith, above her head; a sort of groaning like that which living creatures stifle within themselves when they are going to yield to their passions. She is familiar with it, this groaning that nobody hears. Ennemonde looks at Rachel, who is going peacefully about her tasks, Samuel and Ferdinand who accompany each other in everything and for everything, without fuss or formality. She has a thought for Alithéa and her monkey-tricks, her ridiculous reckonings-up; another thought for the café-owner's wife and even for the schoolteacher. They imagine that night is coming. Yes, night does come, but something else is coming too ! For the present all is calm, it is still winter, but it is foretold that it is coming to an end. Nothing succumbs without a struggle, nothing begins without a struggle. It will be for tomorrow.

She calls, and someone comes to wheel her inside. Samuel and Ferdinand, who have heard her voice, come to the threshold, bang their great shoes against the first tread of the stair, and go up to the kitchen for the time has come—with Rachel and Siméon Chien-loup (who would be vexed to miss the ceremony)—to wash and dress 'la Maman' for the night.

The four of them are none too many. The three men lift her up and carry her to the trestle bed that Rachel had got ready. It is true that Samuel, like Ferdinand or Siméon, could lift a dead weight of a hundred and thirty-five to a hundred and forty kilos unaided; but Ennemonde is not a dead weight, she is a live weight; alive in her gaze (so beautiful still), in her warmth, in the precise intelligence of which she has given many proofs throughout the day and which can be felt to take an interest in the fact that there are three men, two of them her sons, to handle her. This group weighs a good deal more than a hundred and thirty-five to a hundred and forty kilos. At this stage Rachel has gone to empty the pot that was inside the throne. Siméon Chien-loup slips a pillow under Ennemonde's head, under the snow-white hair fine as silk. Siméon loves to touch this hair. Rachel washes it twice a month with some very expensive nonsense that foams and smells of violets (the only perfume Ennemonde likes, apart from that of mignonette). It is two and a half feet long and, freshly washed, so supple that it undulates like snakes. Very pretty hair, Siméon says to himself. At the beginning of these shared attentions Siméon was not entrusted with any important tasks; Samuel and Ferdinand reserved these for themselves; then they saw that Siméon enjoyed it, so there was no longer any reason for excluding him and it was tacitly understood that the pillow under the head was for him, that removing the slippers and pulling off the stockings was naturally for Rachel, that the passing of hands under Ennemonde's buttocks to undo her apron and unfasten her skirt was for Samuel, Ferdinand and Siméon together (six hands), that removing the skirt, the apron, the knitted wool underwear and the pants was again for Rachel, that to steady the belly that then spilled over was for Siméon again on the right side and Samuel again on the left, while Ferdinand took 'Maman's' shoulders in his arms and lifted them so that Rachel could remove her bodice, and so on.

The sequel makes Siméon Chien-loup tremble just a little; oh! not very much—he has seen others—but a trembling in which he cannot easily distinguish what is due to terror and what to pleasure; one must remember that Ennemonde is nearly eighty, that she still has very fine eyes; obviously they had faded at the time she wept so much, then they regained their bloom when she began to take an interest in the family's problems; she has hair whose whiteness is as beautiful as the black it was formerly (which is rare) but still, eighty, as they say, is a good age and has never been famous for the freshness and lustre it gives the flesh. It should be added that, ever since Ennemonde was paralysed (and that's over fifteen years) it has been in process of increasing and embellishment without restraint. It gives the impression that if one did not hold it in handfuls within the frame and extent of the trestle-bed it would spill over on to the floor, it's so abundant. It must be said that it no longer has any definite shape. They are aware (the four who are there—Samuel, Ferdinand, Rachel, Siméon) that it is a woman because of the face, and particularly because of the Christian name, but there is nothing visible to indicate it in the shape of the body, one can only guess. Then, for fear of the sores that might develop in the folds of this flesh, it is washed, powdered with talc, and clean linen applied every evening. After the skirts, the bodice, the underclothes and, especially, an extraordinary pair of zouave pantaloons of fine calico, the three men and Rachel remove Ennemonde's day chemise. Then she is naked.

She is washed. She restrains whoever holds the sponge (it is Samuel or Ferdinand or Siméon, never Rachel, so it has been decided once for all in the deeper meaning of the proceedings). 'Wait a moment,' Ennemonde says. She thinks she has heard something new outside, but it is only the sighing at the time of twilight, nothing that could possibly presage the approach of an upheaval. 'No, go ahead, continue.

'Now it's night, one can no longer tell whether the sky has been bruised over a greater expanse. No sound outside, only the groaning within. It's still winter (at least, that's what they think) but not for long now, and perhaps, even before they've washed my feet. . . .'

She is an old woman waiting for the spring. It will come, never doubt it, it will be here one day or another, soon. She is on the trestle-bed. Shapeless, like a mixture of flour and water and salt, but with a leaven still of great freshness, that is still being kneaded a little tonight but tomorrow will be flattened with a rolling-pin to give it a useful shape. Yes, the spring will come.

II

When mysteries are very evil, they hide in the light; the shade is only a booby-trap. The Camargue is a delta, the refuse-dump of a river, an alcove. Until now it has flowed rapidly without having had the time to indulge in metaphysics, it has lived. In this delta it is near its end, it is going to disappear in the sea, so it languishes, it idles, it recapitulates; everything it has brought this far it ruminates over, mixes up, rots, takes the zest out of.

It turns everything it has torn from its banks into silt, humus and sand. Everything it has killed it exerts itself to resuscitate, all that has died in it it makes alive. The seed so furiously transported here it cajoles, incubates, bursts open.

If it had done this sooner it would have been covered with foliage, but so close to its disappearance in the sea the climate will aid it only with willows and samphire; it is already soda and salt.

Phantoms inhabit this fierce light. A Camarguais Hamlet would encounter his father's ghost at noon. After Christ, the religion of Christ is raised to a pinnacle by the sun. The sign of the Cross is not enough to shelter these vague territories where the four elements mingle. There is need of a vagueness of signs, a multiplicity of motives for hope. As well as the sacrifice of the righteous there is need of the substance of delight and adventure, and it is not so much the cardinal virtues that one blends with the Cross as the sensual and the marine. The Cross, here, is proud of what it bore. It is not ashamed of the blood it drank; it demands more, it has many feasts to perfume. The heart that is erected everywhere as a symbol is a very precise representation of muscle and not of spirit. A charnel-house odour exhales from every tuft of furze; death wears the colours of a peacock. There are no longer any barriers between Heaven and Hell. The immortality of the soul is a clown's grimace to amuse the children; what blazons and spreads in broad daylight is the immortality of the flesh, the immortality of matter, the cycle of transformation, the wheel of life, an infinity of adventures and avatars, the opening out of innumerable paths of flight and glory. The odour of decay that mounts from the roots, the sedge, is the odour of victorious warriors. In place of faith and peace, the pulpits and the plinths bear the sign of the intellect and its struggles.

In the sky of these grey lands, whose colours have been worn by sun and salt to the bare thread, Lucifer-Athene trills like a lark.

Granted, a decent appearance is shown to the century. There is no problem for whoever is satisfied with the superficial; it is a part of a French Department. It has its Prefect and Superintendent of Police, its *gendarmes* and its worthies. It has its Masses and its pilgrimages just like any Brittany, Auvergne or Poland. It has its legal officers. It even has its ceremonial; the sale of postcards and stencils does well out of it. If the sun were to shift ever so little, there would be Camargues in Saintonge. It's enough to broaden the brim of a hat to fill the tourist's heart with Texan heroics; but Dante has only a cap.

Over these vast flat spaces the water circulates at will. It is no longer urged on by gradient and gravity but, so it seems, by intent. It has its avenues, which it covers with reflections, it seems motionless. To catch the shiver of its movement means to be dazzled. It has its streets where it wanders and which it then abandons, so that the earth dries up and cracks like a heart. It has its pools where it sleeps. This is no longer H_2O, but Medusa. It makes this sound of wind in the still air, climbing over the reeds in search of a new path. It flows out over uncovered land. The grey dust smokes before its snout, it is a snake that grows, advances, and devours the land. The sun covers it with black gold. Blind, but heavy with primeval forces, it rises, coils, metamorphoses under your eyes, heedless of your Christian certainties, your political beliefs and your scientific future; it brings with it the elements of illusion from which the gods are generated spontaneously. Even he who steps back slowly, steps back; even he who knows, knows only the escape routes.

Not that this water threatens you with sudden death, it is not deep, it is not rapid, don't run away, it will hardly wet your feet. It does not threaten your soul. It will only destroy your essence. Your classification becomes a pandemonium, your physics and chemistry poetry. What, till now, you based on M. Eiffel you must henceforth base on M. Wave.

Often, in these expanses of bronze covered with reeds, one can hear the splashing passage of some invisible animal; one listens, names come to mind: fox? badger? boar? None is satisfactory. Horse? ox? Minotaur? Its sound is at once heavy and light, is it the winged lion of the Assyrian murals? One looks: the sky has lightened, the sun pours down only a grey light, it is as if the rushes of the marsh were riven by some antediluvian form. The sound of its approach fills the whole expanse. This creature is so enormous and unnameable that the day is sick with it, the calendar shrivels up on itself. There is no more space; one seems to be looking at some internal landscape; no more time, one has been watching, immobile, for eternity. The beast prowls; it is over there, it is here. It is in my heart, it is in the blackness of the marshes, it approaches, it moves away. It cannot be seen, only its track. It seeks no prey (what use would human flesh be to such an important beast?). It seeks a goal and one knows that one is the white of the target. The Andromeda myth opens a thousand icy corridors in the most everyday soul. The odour rises: the odour of mud (we are in a delta), of fish, but so eloquent that the entire vast sky is nothing but the eye of the fish, that one imagines its scales touching the galaxies, that its tail recedes into the far corners of the world in an expansion faster than light. An odour of decay, but as bland to the spirit as the odour of mushrooms is bland to the taste; a formidable odour of birth before form, at the moment when life mingled with death still has the right to choose what it will become. Odour of reptiles, of the first vertebrates that do not yet know how to hold themselves upright. Odour of everything it has been necessary to strive against for thousands of centuries to succeed in no longer touching the ground save with the soles of the feet. The mastodon we await seems wiser than all the Churches. We are not afraid of its ferocity, we are afraid of its affection. It has not yet revealed itself and already, with its noise and its stink, it has destroyed us and recreated us in inverse fashion, bit by bit, and especially upside-down. We fear the contagion of its shape; especially we fear having no name to designate this shape (which is going to be our own) and being drawn (at our age! in our position! in our family situation! with the place we hold! being what we are!) into a truant school of sensibility. Nothing is more agitating than the odour of the stirred-up mud. Still those rushes oscillating in its track, which now comes nearer. The beast is going to come into the open. The rushes separate, it breaks cover! We are face-to-face with all that is inhuman that one has been able to discover in oneself (and that is a good deal). Nothing happens; except, perhaps, the passage of an invisible body in the height of the sky. It moves away (just as we become ashamed of the weapons in our hands) and goes to be submerged in the Mediterranean. In the south we hear the clamour of the sea.

But it is a time when everything grows quiet. The clouds extend and redden in the sunset; they are motionless over the hills beyond Nîmes and Uzès. They are already asleep. Here the stream gurgles. The shade spreads disquiet but romanticism expands in the fear of the inhabited glades. The phantoms move away with the sun. A long green grasshopper carefully rehearses the triggering of its thighs. One can see it pondering its leap. It kneads the dust with its little claws, it turns its Philippe Augustus head to every side, it measures the depth of the air with its antennae, buries its face in its knees, and at last it jumps, opens its red wings and drops down again at a spot exactly like the one it has just left. Swarms of flies are like widows' veils in flight. Flights of mosquitoes as thick as tigers whet their claws against the silken air. The plunging of the frogs adds a dimension to the night. The owl quivers its feathers from bush to bush. The nightjar hums. Somewhere a wader croaks. And this is also the hour of the actual fox, less visible than its ghost; but it barks, and its domestic contentions add volume to the night. Rats flee the dangers of rats, pursue the prey of rats, or dream those rats' dreams in which they race in a pack, belly to ground. The last gleam of daylight brightens with the swoop of the last swallow. The first star lights up. The brazier of towns and villages illuminates the curved horizon of the plain. One can hear the murmur of the great arm of the Rhône. The fish slap the surface of the pools. Towards Aigues-Mortes the melancholy cry of the herons tunnels the night. The silence has a Roman eloquence. Everything that's alive stirs and moves noiselessly, even the reeds, even the stunted trees. The stars invade the delta. There are more constellations in the Vaccarès than in the sky. The mud and rottenness smell like Turkish delight. Love and slaughter having the same sound, it seems that all matter is in process of loving. The illusions of the night use the language of the nursery. One hears horses neigh, oxen bellow, but no one knows if these herd noises come from the land or from the sea, stirred in its depths and rubbing against the sands.

The red of the sun lingers in Piedmont, here there throbs the greatest dawn imaginable, night has not yet departed from the lanes of Arles but, already, a light as of snow imposes its reflections on the waste expanses. The sea itself is still dark. Towards Miramas, Salon and around the lake at Berre, where the land is just as bare, where the sheets of water are vaster and nearer to the east, the dawn is still blue; here, reflected by the sands, it has suddenly assumed extraordinary whiteness. At Avignon the swallows hardly poke a beak out of the nest, here they turn and creak in the bitter sky. From the first ray of the sun feathers blaze on all sides : the black of the wagtail, the red of the stonechat, the plover's yellow and the grey of the sandpiper, the green of the lapwing and the godwit's red, the grey of the curlew and the white of the merganser as well as the orange sheldrake and the scoter duck that circles in flights of blue wool over the marshes. All that flies, all that scampers, all that crawls is on the move. While the sun climbs the Alps in the east, a rapid transient life begins here in the Camargue. The night, in which murders are committed in a half-slumber, flees towards the Cévennes; the African day that inflames the blood is not yet here. The wild sow, followed by her young boars, leaves her lair. Only the white streak these creatures bear on their back can be seen, the rest of their coat is the colour of earth. Flights of waders cross the marshes like maple seeds borne by the wind. The green lizard emerges from the ditches, it advances on the sand at its sleepwalker's pace, it runs at full speed or suddenly stops, petrified, without reason. This is the *guilleret* or *guillevert*. Some assert that it has a terrible bite, others that it is the companion of Diana and that it warns the sleeping hunter of the viper's approach by crawling over his belly. It is the king of catalepsy; in mid-career, in the middle of a leap, it becomes fixed, petrified in marble immobility. Only its eyes remain alive. When it fights it is like a cat. It rounds its back by rising on its feet, it lowers its head, it scolds silently, that is, instead of raising its voice anger makes it threaten in a feebler and feebler murmur until, silently, it leaps on its adversary. It is as green as if the colour green had just been invented for it at that moment. The zoologists say that it assumes a spectral posture. The truth is that it sees the gods! The gods of this land are monsters. I don't mean that they are diplodoci, but simply that they are not to be understood by Cartesian reasoning. Christ, Buddha, Mohammed and all the ophidians of the Aztecs are only the viscera of these gigantic gods.

The coronella or smooth snake leaves its hole. It is the most intelligent of serpents. It too sees God with its small milky eye that seems blind, but it does not go into a trance for so little. It is a Chinaman, it spends its day writing ideograms on the sands.

And here is the warrior: the *zaménis*, or green and yellow snake, also called the lashing or whip snake because of its long slender tail. This snake easily measures a metre to a metre and a half in overall length. It is arrogant and full of initiative, it climbs trees, it pillages nests, it has a brisk and savage nature, it bites furiously. The *guillevert* alone stands up to it, leaps at its throat, and sees it off. Others it swallows naked and raw, alive. It loves to feel its prey dying slowly, struggling and even clawing against its extensile gullet. Its greed is for the agony of others. It loves, not just to feed on them, but to enjoy them. It will have nothing to do with what is inert; but as soon as it spies something living nearby, it thinks (for it thinks) how delightful it would be to ingest this life. It is a shrewd creature. Its digestion is Caesarian. It has two penises armed with recurved spines which make separation difficult, often fatal, when it grapples. The female must either die or kill the male and devour him (which, nine times out of ten, she prefers to do).

There is much to be said about the snakes. There are the two great snakes made by the river which entwine this region. There are the marshes, the sand, the tangled vegetable flotsam, the atrocious heat, the blinding light, these invisible gods. It is the geometric haunt of the serpent.

At this hour, when the sun is still in process of painfully climbing the eastern slopes of the Alps, all that flies, all that crawls, all that jumps thrives on the white light of the dawn. It is a ceremonial moment. They exult in the glory of their feathers, their coats, their scales. As yet, they do not exist; it is their essence that momentarily sets them in motion.

The grass snake, or ladies' snake: large head, short snout, great eyes, round pupil, yellow iris, an eye from which the light seems to emerge as if the rest of the world were the eye and this eye the thing seen. The female is a gross creature, and the one most often seen; she is a metre in length (on average; in some cases she reaches two metres or more), she is thick, she does not creep in indecipherable ideograms like the coronella, she drags herself along. She is not a scholar but a housewife. Her male is slenderer and smaller, one would not think they were the same species; he wriggles, he is olive-coloured, sometimes blue; he bears the decoration of the Golden Fleece—a white collar supporting an orange triangle. The grass snake does not bite, hence its name of ladies' snake. But it frightens by its size, its muscle, its ferocious appearance, its eye that rejects the world's spectacle and considers itself the spectacle of this world. It might be thought that this is why it does not bite. On the other hand, the ladies' snake has the habit of sprinkling the nauseating secretions of its cloacal glands and its excreta copiously on whoever lays hold of it. They are few. It is enormous and readily assumes a ferocious aspect. It ingests its prey starting from the hinder parts, so as to leave it plenty of time to scream. It enjoys these screams. Despite its bulk it is a beautiful animal in the morning, when it is not yet hunting and displays its beauty. It can be seen in the tracks the water has abandoned, or on the edges of the marshes where the mud begins. No one ever throws stones at it because there is no chance of killing it with blows from a stone. It must be killed with a stick or a rifle. This snake, whatever its nature, is so simply and entirely beautiful that man kills it for pleasure.

Let us return to the birds while we speak of beauty.

There are thousands, of all species, of every plumage, of all colours. There's not a lost island of the far Atlantic that does not send here its northern gannet, its scamew, its pigmy seagull, its sea swallow or black tern. The cormorant, the tufted merganser, the Miquelon long-tailed duck, the diver, the lapwing, the sandpiper, the turnstone, the common sandpiper, mingle their red, green, blue, yellow, orange, black, pure white and that iris grey in which all other colours dissolve in a thousand turns of flight. Even the six-plumed bird of paradise known by the name of *sifilet*, wearing on either side of its head three narrow and extraordinarily prolonged feathers and with a beautiful emerald gloss on its flanks, which comes here to act the musketeer and twirl its moustache. Some are reputed to live only in remote Siberias; they are here. Others, like the golden-headed trogon or the blue chatterer need the swamps and alli-gator rivers, yet here they are in this country of bare sands, reeds and little lizards. There is even the turacos, or plantain-eater, a phoenix-like red bird that loses its colour in the water. If the turacos gets wet and rubs itself in the sand, the sand becomes red and the turacos white; but as soon as it dries it turns red again. These same phenomena cannot be repeated with the dead dried skin of the bird. There are swifts, quail, cranes, storks, geese, a thousand varieties of duck, all migrants and travellers who come here to moult and regrow their plumage. Some—from the blackest to the rosiest—come from the forests, there are the birds from the steppes, from the shores of the Lena, from the shores of the Amou-Daria, those from the Euphrates, from the Silk

Road, from Kerguelen and Newfoundland. There is a colony of some hundreds of finches from Punta Arenas; and Magellan's grouse planes in the pure blue of the sky as it planes distractedly in the storms and tumults of the Beagle Canal. The curlew of the glaciers fraternizes with the stonechat. The cowbirds and orioles of America build their nests here as they do in the tropics, in the shape of a retort to protect their brood from climbing mammals. Some hollows in the dunes contain the nests of the gold-ringed widow-bird, which never contain any eggs, and those of the black guan, which are full to overflowing. And then there are the natives, the locals, the skulkers that haunt the stubble and the heaths, from Carpentras to Montpellier, from Sète to Marseilles, from Vauvert to Lambesc : the cuckoo, the greenfinch, the great tit, the coal-tit, the wagtail . . . the finch, the blackbird, the robin, the thrush, the nightingale, the goldfinch, the bullfinch, the lark, the magpie, and, last, the sparrow, the good Gallic sparrow, the laziest of birds, who lives in human company, swarms in the cities, and keeps its idle city-dweller habits here.

All these aliens and these natives mingle their flights and their cries in the morning. Every throat swallows and harmoniously expels this air, tasting of marshes and mystery. Those with a cylindrical windpipe emit the sounds of the flute, fife and flageolet; those with a conical windpipe, narrower toward the base than at the beak, boom like an organ sounding. Some utter the calls of horns, trumpets or trombones; others strike on crystal strings or set drums vibrating. The canary, the greenfinch and the oriole sing their love-songs. The sparrows

set up a plaintive clamour at the sight of a shrike. Everywhere the air resounds with whistlings, gurglings of
tenderness or disquiet. The sedge-warbler raises its voice
to compete with the nightingale. The passerines intone
their especial song, a song of war and terror; the guttural
note of the bullfinch strikes the smooth surface of the
lakes with such force as to make it shiver; the carnivorous birds, with their more tapering beaks, sigh more
tenderly than any, their notes are more passionate, more
enchanting, while they spy around them with the
extreme brightness of cruel unintelligent eyes. The crying birds of the open seas, constructed to call to each
other over long distances amid the sound of the waves,
arouse the expanses of reeds and still water with their
heavy wings and their clamour.

At last, at a single bound, the sun leaps into the delta
from the summit of the Alps. Suddenly all is silent, all
the flights subside, all the birds creep into the bushes,
go to earth under tufts of spurge, slip under the reeds, drop
anchor in the most shadowy marshes. At one moment
the surface of every waterway seethes with the reflection
of all these wings, is streaked with the furrows of these
flying armadas, then it becomes smooth and empty once
more, a mirror showing only sun and sky. Silence. Then,
with the day, the serpent-eater appears on the scene. He
arrives with rapid steps, which is why he is called the
messenger; he has his pen over his ear like a Civil Service
clerk, which is why he is also called the secretary bird.
He does not use his wings to speed his rapid course; he
uses his ferocity, which he hardens like a bullet in the
head that he darts in front, dashing headlong like a

Greek hero. He strides over the sands like Achilles about Troy. He is a walking vulture designed to live in deserts. He lives in the midst of the Iliad. His legs are sheathed in armour. He is as grey as an old warrior, save for his flanks where, like ancient trophies of rapine, he wears emerald, sapphire and tarnished gold. For a long time he has been searching for snakes. He was waiting for the biggest. He awaited the sun. The sun is here, he waits no longer, he attacks. It is usually a big grass snake, thick as a man's arm, which stops still, distends its neck, and whistles terrifyingly. In the nearby bushes everything hides and goes to earth. The serpent-eater spreads one of his wings and holds it in front of him, like a shield covering his legs. The snake darts; the bird leaps, strikes, throws itself backward, jumps in every direction and resumes the struggle, always presenting his shield of feathers; and while the snake exhausts itself striking and biting at this soft grey apron, the bird detaches it with vigorous blows from its other wing. The bewildered reptile wavers and tries to escape. The serpent-eater breaks its head with strokes of its beak and drinks its brains; it dances a little ritual dance round the still moving corpse, hopping on one foot, beating its wings, tossing its head agitatedly like a horse doing the Spanish step; finally he completely skins his victim and swallows it in great chunks. Replete, he closes his eyes as if in sleep, drunk with food, satiated ferocity, and logic.

If I have spoken of this play-acting it is because, as in every country of the sun, we are in the midst of a general dramaturgy. Beneath the river's accumulated silt the skeleton of ancient glacial moraines raises little islands of firm ground above the marshes and submerged land. On these islands there are built those small white houses with thatched or tiled roofs that are to be found in every delta and estuary, in the mouths of the Odiel and the Rio Tinto and of the Guadalquivir. These little houses, so much like lumps of sugar, exhibit all the features of remote dwellings designed for a single inhabitant; a recluse, I ought to say. This architecture (of great simplicity : four walls, white-washed inside and out, and a roof) is not eloquent of wife and family. Nor of a home. It's quite the opposite of an English home. There is no question here, as in the rainy countries, of an everlasting conjugal atmosphere. The only luxuries here are shade and siesta. The four walls and the roof provide the shade; that is all they are needed for (and the siesta is always available). Actually, they are needed for rather more, as everywhere else; but while, in the lands of perpetual twilight, one needs not only a home but also to make it attractive, here it's enough to paint the walls a pure, dazzling white, so that in the dazzle this white produces the shade will prove more dark. And that suffices, simply because of the theatre the sun creates in every avenue of feeling.

Direct theatre, based on blood; and on violence, since this is the most direct way to obtain blood. In countries where the light is grey the slower passage of time facilitates the engendering of diplomacy, and hence of society; the countries of the sun live faster, conduce to violence and solitude. This rapidity of life engenders the lie. Not the opposite of the truth but the generalized lie, that is to say the creation of a new truth.

This is the human condition of the inhabitants of these little sugar-lump houses. And in our times, when money is made out of everything, we must distinguish between the genuine inhabitants, who are very few (and almost invisible) and the false, who are numerous (and very obvious).

I used to know one of these authentic Camarguais. He was a man devoid of any picturesque externals. He did not have a big hat or a carefully knotted scarf; he did not wear a sheriff's boots; he did not know how to strike a pose before the camera and when he laughed he displayed a toothless mouth (due to raw leeks, not to garlic, not that that's any better). He was not attractive. He spoke exactly like everyone else, that is French with a very strong meridional accent. He climbed on a horse so marvellously that he gave the miserable impression of a bumpkin in an armchair. On his mount he did not evoke the brave deputies of the Far West, or any circus riders, but a kind of equestrian proletariat; he sat his horse like a workman at his bench. He did not mount to play to the gallery or to make an impression, he mounted for himself and to watch cattle. He cared more for his buttocks than for the spectators. As he had a definite job to do, and this job required him to be on horseback twelve hours a day, and, as he did this job for over thirty years, he had adopted, not the most elegant manner of sitting in the saddle, but the most comfortable.

He had a cap (like everybody's), an old cloth coat (a

double-breasted blue worsted coat that had seen its best days in 1913), long trousers, and espadrilles. He also had a brave little stomach, of the kind called *brioche*, and a habit of chewing tobacco, which was not the best thing for his breath.

As to his genuineness, that was beyond dispute. He was the last descendant of a long line of ancestors, all bachelors, who had lived at Mas-Thibert or the surroundings. These recluses lived their solitary lives in the shadow of a carefully maintained genealogical tree. My authentic Camarguais was called Louis, had no surname, or claimed not to have one, and could trace his lineage back to his greatgrandfather. The birth of that distant progenitor was lost in the night of time. All that was certain was that in 1823 he was cattle-herd on behalf of one Adolphe Émeric, that on the very place where he kept herd he had built the house shaped like a lump of sugar that Louis still lived in in 1959. As well as the house there remained another relic of this individual, whom Louis called 'the old man'; this was a small tricolour flag bearing the embroidered words: 'Liberty or Death'. A relic of the *coup d'état* of '51. In '51 'the old man' who, according to Louis's statements, must have been sixty to sixty-five years old, found in the neighbourhood of a place called the *bac du Sauvage* the body of a small man half hidden in the reeds. After extricating him from the marsh he recognized a butcher's apprentice from Bellegarde, and saw that he was still breathing despite having his nostrils blocked by mud. He cleared his nostrils, carried the little man back to the hut, and looked after him. The little butcher's body had been wrapped in this flag. When he could speak (which happened soon enough, as he very much wanted to) he told 'the old man' that, as a member of the insurgent forces, he had been pursued by regular troops and had tried to swim across an arm of the Rhône but that, buffeted by the water, he had become exhausted and finally lost consciousness. The old man returned the butcher's boy to general circulation and the rebel left the flag at the cowherd's. The *bac du Sauvage* was a haulage ferry managed by one of those muscular cripples who have been the joy of romantics since Quasimodo. Though this one was neither hunchbacked nor one-eyed, he nevertheless had legs like coatsleeves and cork-screw shoulders. Nothing gave any indication of his strength and he was as strong as a Turk. He lived not very far from the spot where 'the old man' had found the little butcher, in a house equally like a lump of sugar, but hidden in a thicket of tall green reeds.

The butcher's boy had raised certain problems in the simple mind of the cowherd, notably this: 'How could it happen that a person lucky enough to pursue a career as attractive as that of a butcher should try to cross the Rhône, with a tricolour flag wrapped round his body?'

This was insoluble; and to find some certainty (and likewise to revisit the scene of his exploit) the old man often came to loiter by the ferry.

The aquatic Quasimodo had a daughter as quasi-modesque as himself. She was getting on for thirty-five or forty and, for over twenty years, despite the strange construction of her body and thanks to the milky skin that always attracts strong men, she had beguiled the leisure hours of all who were worthwhile from Port-Saint-Louis-du-Rhône to Le Grau-du-Roi. She had had a rabble of children who, at the proper time, got drowned, died of croup, choked themselves swallowing cherries, or managed to survive, fishing for frogs, swimming like tunnies, etc. Though aware of all this, the old man had never seen this dream creature at close quarters. He saw her. This was in May. During the Carnival of the following year, while they were sounding the trumpets for Ash Wednesday, the ferryman's daughter came to bring the old man a little boy, quite new, and not at all badly made. According to her, this was their son; according to him, it was a possibility. She added that she did not wish to keep this one in the common flock because he had red hair (and indeed it did really seem that his down was red). The old man never went against Nature. This desire seemed natural to him. He looked after the child, that is, he bedded it on some sacks in a corner of his hut and went on herding his cattle on horseback for the rest of his time. But whenever he got back (sometimes after ten hours of riding through the storm), he always found the little one tidy, fed and smiling, or bawling like a calf but from sheer pleasure. And so for two or three years (but three years, that's fantastic!) until the day when the ferryman's daughter was blown to pieces by a boxful of black powder with which she was fishing, just under the bridge at Beaucaire, in the company, as it happened, of a gipsy to whom she was purveying illicit delights. This premature explosion set the old man on the sentimental track. He had never believed in the Holy Ghost from

seeing the child cared for by mysterious hands; as soon
as he heard of the accident at Beaucaire he looked at the
boy's mouth and said to himself : 'It's up to me to fill it
now.' The boy had not had red hair after all (nor the
old man either), the old man had realized this from the
earliest days (there were no flies on him, they had col-
oured his fluff with birds' feathers; but it was precisely
this ruse of the mother that persuaded the old man that
it really was his son—always, of course, without exag-
gerating, the old man wasn't one for exaggeration). He
called his horse Bicou, he called the child Bicou, and to
hell with it.

The winter of 1875 was a terrible one. No one had
ever known such cold. The mistral never abated; one
could hardly put one's nose out of doors. The old man
rode round as best he could to look for his animals,
which became drowsy with the cold and went to lie
down and die on the dunes. The pools froze instan-
taneously round the feet of the ducks; one had only to
break the ice to pick up the birds. Like all men of the
sun, the old man allowed himself to be seduced by the
temptation of the cold. He clearly preferred death to
life, and, having coughed a great deal (a cough that
strangely resembled the melancholy voice of oxen lost
in the night), he lay stiff and stark on his camp-bed.

Bicou was twelve years old. During the last week he
had guarded the herd unaided; a fortnight after the
old man's death, and while the corpse was mummifying
with cold in the house, shut up like a tomb, which
Bicou never re-entered, the child was managing the herd
with a master-hand. The owner (who had changed—it

was no longer Adolphe Émeric, who was *deceased*, but his eldest son Jules, who had had his fair share of trouble in dividing the property with his sisters and brothers-in-law), the owner of the herd did not learn of the old man's death until July. By this time Bicou had long since abandoned the grassy hollow where he used to dwell and reopened the door of the little sugar-lump house; he had long since buried in the sand the carcass of the old man, scrupulously cleaned and emptied by swarms of bees. Jules Émeric sent a man from Vauvert to herd the cattle. The latter arrived one Wednesday morning; on the Wednesday evening his horse returned alone to Mas-Thibert. The man from Vauvert was discovered alive but dazed, stunned, flattened like an omelette across a door. He did not know what had happened to him. He had a hole at the back of his head, probably made by a stone. He must have injured himself in a fall from his horse. Jules Émeric sent a man from Lunel. The man from Lunel's horse returned alone and the man from Lunel was discovered alive but dazed, stunned, flattened like an omelette across a door. As for learning what had happened to him? Nothing. According to him, nothing had happened to him. He had heard the buzzing of a big fly. He too had a hole at the back of his head. Jules Émeric sent a type from Nîmes. This chap, forewarned, was on his guard. So much so that he was found flat out like the others. The people of Nîmes being renowned for their intelligence, they paid attention to what the man said; he said that, in his opinion, there was a sling thereabouts swung by a master-hand. Jules Émeric entrusted the care of the

E

herd to Bicou. He had noticed that the cattle obeyed the child's voice as one man; he also thought that, besides, a child was paid much less than a man; finally, since this child had a sling, it was as well to reckon with it.

Whether from true heredity or from habits acquired during long years of living together, Bicou very much resembled 'the old man' in character. His herd came first or, more exactly, the pleasure of living on horseback behind his cattle came first. But he took after his mother in certain extravagances of behaviour—skill with a sling was one, liking for company another. It wasn't so much a matter of human company as of company in general; and, especially at the time of his puberty and adolescence, Bicou associated with communities of cattle, birds, small mammals, reeds (particularly when the marsh quivered in the evening breeze) and even minerals. He knew that one is never bored, even with a piece of granite, if one allows oneself to consider it solidly for hours. He was not, in principle, opposed to meeting people, to associating with them as he associated with granite and wild life; in any case he had no principles and if he did try it a little later, naturally without the least blend of metaphysics, he found such company less pleasant than the other. He had inherited a Herculean strength from his maternal grandfather, people were always on at him to make him show off; he did not like being a show and there was nothing to see with other people. When, as was his habit, he lengthily considered a man or woman, not only did he learn very little but the subject ended up by getting annoyed or teasing him.

This need for solitude and for company made him

facile in the art of basket-making. When he plaited the willow he had the feeling of masterful involvement in society and of shaping it to his will. The great moral satisfaction that he thus drew from his work led him to invent new forms of weaving. He possessed in his fingers an audacity of eloquence, insinuation and suppleness; he was the Cicero of the basket. And so, though he remained silent, his discourse was spread about the countryside. Carried away by this mode of self-expression, he perfected it in every moment of his life. He knew all the resources of the region; his long rides with the cattle, his power of communion with all creation, animal, vegetable, mineral, gave him access to an extraordinary collection of methods of expression. He knew where to find the spiny rest-harrow, from which a golden dye can be made; the bindweed soldanella or sea-cabbage, whose sap mixed with salt replaces purple; the herbaceous starwort, the round-leaved pirole, and the bog-myrtle which, crushed with mussel-shell, makes perfect black. He had learned to gauge the colours, to make them indelible with hedge-hog gall, to tell the age of the osiers, and to choose those boughs whose fibres were supple enough to permit him, with an economy of means, a fine style full of private satisfaction; he knew how to varnish his work with a decoction of the pulicaria, or herb of St Roch; in short, through his personal magic, by simply following his bent, he had made himself desirable.

Returning home one evening, he discovered, unharnessed near his house, what at Lunel, Aigues-Mortes, Saint-Gilles, Vauvert and even Nîmes, was called a *carrosse*. This was a gilded cart, the rear of which was a raised platform, as in the boats used for jousting. This platform was draped in red and surrounded by a balustrade in imitation marble of the 'garden of love' variety; hung on this balustrade, like seaweed on Thetis's chariot, were two hunting-horns, two trombones and a cornet. The drum was invisible. This vehicle conveyed to the townships, villages and farms a personage whom some called Casagrande, others Diablon, who was a gipsy. He extracted teeth to the sound of an orchestra. To this art he added that of manufacturing worm-powders, he stole chickens, told fortunes vaguely, and besides this was a basket-maker. Or if not he, himself, then his wives, of whom he had seven, two of whom were always pregnant in rotation. The brats blew into the bugles and beat the drum to drown the cries of the patients, the girls sold baskets and so-called handmade lace that came from the factories at Nancy. Casagrande, of uncertain age, thin, dried-up, dark, glossy, had turned-up moustaches that made the corners of his mouth bitter even when he smiled.

Casagrande thought it advisable to use diplomacy in learning Bicou's secrets and had prepared his weapons accordingly. In his role as head of the tribe he had decided to hazard the charms of his youngest wife, with whom he did not get on well in any case. This young woman, named Myriam, in whose blood were mingled a number of Macedonians and other Balkanians, had only submitted to Casagrande's yoke in obedience to the sumptuary laws of her race; in reality, she aimed higher than a tooth-puller, without clearly realizing at what, and she was looking around for standards of comparison so as to arrange her future knowledgeably. It happened that she was not pregnant that year but, given her character, she ran the risk of not remaining in this state for long. There was no time to lose; Casagrande did not hesitate and before arriving to install himself by Bicou's white hut he had indoctrinated Myriam at length with the short-handled whip he used to bullyrag his mule. Now she was prepared.

But it was unnecessary, for Bicou, like every great orator, was far from making any mystery of his methods. Moreover, he was attracted by Myriam, or, more exactly, in revenge for the mule whip Myriam did everything to make herself attractive.

Casagrande remained in the neighbourhood of the little sugar-lump house for three years. From time to time he went off to pull a few teeth and sell (what was now) de luxe basket-work, then returned; Bicou's secrets were a gold-mine, and innumerable. At last, one fine day, he decamped. He was not to return.

Bicou understood; the preceding day someone had stolen his knife, which is always a sign of a definitive rupture of an association. It was child's play for him to catch up with the cart at the Beaucaire bridge. He made Myriam hand over the little girl she had had these three months since. They insulted him in the usual manner, by casting doubts on his virility, but they gave him the little girl. Before crossing to the other side of the river Myriam gave him to understand that she had stolen the knife herself, deliberately, to warn him. She still could not forgive Casagrande the whipping, especially with a mule whip, and she was delighted that a girl who might have been put to many uses in a few years time should escape his clutches.

For Bicou she was a sheet-anchor. Three years association with the tribe of the cart had made him lose his taste for minerals, plants, and even animals. The strong odour of the women and their rabble of brats was an intoxicating vapour that turned his head; there was in Casagrande everything that Sunday villages look for in bezique. In memory of the woman who had been capable of anything and yet, on certain occasions, had cooed like a dove, he called the little girl Myriam.

Myriam had her fill of everything that goes to make men : a rough life and vast horizons, silence and natural law, desire and solitude; but she remained a woman. She wasn't a beauty, nor was her mother; her father was like anyone else, so. . . . But health had not been measured to her sparingly. By the nature of things she dressed as a man up to the age of thirty : where would she have found skirts in the early part of her life? She had to use Bicou's trousers; later she got into the habit of dressing like a woman because she had Louis.

She had Louis by deliberate intent, as one buys an object of prime necessity. When she worked it out she found that she had spent more than twenty years with her backside on a saddle, something that gives a woman a good foundation, preserves her from a certain flightiness, and generally inclines her towards the pleasurable arts.

But we anticipate; Bicou had a regal death. One night he did not return and Myriam, who was twenty-

five then, found a large assembly of cattle at a place
called La Jouquelle. It was in the middle of the night;
Myriam was on a white mare which became frantic,
but which she soon brought to her senses. With bloodstained flanks and mouth the mare, sidling and reluc-
tant, approached the enormous herd, darker than the
night, from which there issued a muffled modulated
rumbling, as a cat might purr if it were a kilometre
long. There were cattle there who did not know Myriam;
but those who did know her came to meet her and,
escorting her on right and left, helped her penetrate like
a Caesar into the holy of holies of the assembly. Gripped
by thighs of iron, the mare did not flinch; Myriam
carried a hurricane lamp on her saddlebow.

It was in the heart of this assemblage (and in the red
glow of the lantern), and in the presence of a hundred
oxen, bellowing, muzzles to ground, that she found her
dead father. She brought him back to the house, all the
cattle following; they broke up their procession on
nearing an inhabited place. Bicou bore no wound; he
only had a purplish face and his tongue protruded like
a hanged man's. He had simply been touched by the
finger of God, what our modern medical terminology
calls a myocardial infarction, but this is how it looks
from Sirius.

The owner of the herd (it wasn't Émeric any more,
he had sold it, it was a citizen of Marsillargues), looked
on the bright side of things and left the animals in the
care of the 'young man'. He did not know that Myriam
was a woman. Neither did she.

She found this out, not as one normally does, but

through her reaction to solitude. She had no desire to plait withies. She tried it, as she had tried it when her father was alive, but, having only herself to satisfy now, without success. She dallied in the company of the heifers but was too sensible to share their melancholy.

One autumn evening, when the animals were quiet, she saddled a fresh horse for a fast run and by five o'clock she was in the cypress fields over at Cavaillon. She planned her moves, took the appropriate steps, made numerous calculations in the twinkling of an eye. She bought a skirt and a bodice in a haberdasher's for six francs at Plan d'Orgon and returned home.

As the autumn progressed she made the same trip on several occasions. She tied up her horse in the shade of the cypresses, dressed as a woman in the heart of a thicket of green reeds, and went off to make an appearance near a farm that grew early vegetables. She had chosen the time when the males of this region are at a loose end and smoke cigarettes dolefully in the roads, while kicking at stones. She got off with one of these, a field worker whom she found amenable because he was of uncertain age and had plenty of hair on his face. She had chosen well for he was not surprised, but he demanded forty francs. Nothing could have reassured Myriam more, that was how she saw things, but she did not have forty francs (it was a very large sum). She promised to return and he promised to wait.

And, in fact, he did wait; he waited more than a month while Myriam scoured the fairs and fêtes in boy's clothes in search of her forty francs. In every little village, hamlet or even large stock-farm they used to have an 'ox-run'. This consisted of choosing young, intact and mettlesome animals, fixing a rosette between the two horns, and promising five francs, sometimes six, to whomever could remove the rosette. The animals joined in the game, like animals, by striking out with their horns; the men played with cunning, agility and audacity.

Myriam brought to this game something her father had taught her, that is, a charm. Not in attitude or gracefulness—the young men were a thousand times more supple than she was—but a sort of 'ox language' that she murmured under her breath when approaching the beast. She picked up ten, twenty, then thirty francs in this way. She found it rather more trying to get from thirty to forty for autumn was coming to an end, and the fairs with it. There was one final one when they loosed the meanest oxen in creation. Myriam, who wouldn't have asked for any allowance for anything in the world, took more risks than usual and nearly got herself killed. Her courage, the origin of which was unknown to the spectators, sent everyone into raptures.

So she brought off her affair, but she did not notify her boss until after the birth of the child (whom she called Louis). The citizen of Marsillargues raised his arms to heaven to see his drover in skirts. It was necessary to show him the child, and even to suckle it in his presence, to convince him. He raised his arms to heaven once more and sent a chap from Arles to look after the herd.

The chap from Arles amused himself with the child. A few months later he amused himself with the mother, but this was an enterprise of a very different kind from the one of the forty francs; in any event, Louis never had any brothers or sisters.

In 1944 Louis came out of prison. He had served two months preventive detention as the result of a dirty trick; he was innocent, it had taken two months to discover this. Any sensible man would have seen it before. But Louis was not well-liked in the delta. He was not the only one; he was one of that class of citizens attached to tradition. Now there are several kinds of tradition, two at any rate—the true and the false. There are the traditions that spring from the need to live, there are the traditions that spring from the need to seem. Those who practise the second do not love those who practise the first; and they are generally more skilful.

Anyway, Louis didn't make anything of it. He did not take himself for a Silvio Pellico; he had eaten his haricot beans and lentils with an excellent appetite, he climbed into the saddle again like a bag of dirty washing and went jogging off into his desert, which was no longer so completely deserted, though Louis knew many places where it still was.

Louis took after his grandfather Bicou and his mother; he must also have acquired something from the forty franc father known only to Myriam. On second thoughts, he also inherited Quasimodo's physical strength. It must be admitted, though, that this strength was not apparent and that Louis, even in the flower of his youth, would never have passed for a beach Apollo, but . . . but he could tear up a pack of thirty-two cards with his fingers, which isn't too bad. A strength which he never used, except to halt his horse by closing his thighs, or for calling his herd to order. He measured himself against oxen, never against men. This strength of Quasimodo's, allied to the physical alacrity with which the first Myriam had been endowed, worked wonders during Louis's adolescence.

He seemed to have been imprinted by the severe tasks his mother had imposed on herself to ensure his birth. The fashion for tournaments, where one confronted oxen with a rosette between their horns, had spread to a degree where it might easily have been taken for a tradition. All round the Mediterranean there are always the ambitious that would like to be traced back to Minos; to have the Minotaur in one's blood goes well with idleness. And as there was idleness almost everywhere this kind of nobility, which eliminated the need to trace oneself back to the Crusades, attracted plenty of people. The 'ox-tourney' became a sort of fad for an entire public on the look-out for exotic distractions with a State—that is, a Homeric—backing, for it was a question of a state of mind. The sort of runs that up to then had been organized by simple peasants with few distractions were henceforward organized by licensed organizers. Although, during Louis's adolescence, there still remained unsullied runs where everyone joined in the fête, it became more and more a spectacle given by professionals before a seated audience (who had paid for their seats).

Increasingly, people who were in the habit of taking bladders for lanterns came to sit round cockaded bulls. What had originally been merely a manifestation of proletarian skill had become a machine to satisfy the romanticism of a primary aristocracy. Louis would have been greatly astonished (and Myriam even more) to be informed that people dilated at length, not only on their courage, but on the symbolism of their courage. True, it took plenty of courage to face the bulls, who were fiery, and their horns, which were pointed, but it only took courage for the professionals. It is clear that these last, who postured before the bull like a locksmith before his vice, had a very definite idea of the danger they ran, but Louis! For him it was a matter of passion, and passion leaves no room for calculation. He was paid, where in reality he would have paid, to leap into the arena. When he evaded a horn with a simple swerve of his hip it was not to save his liver or his spleen, it was simply to obey the essence of all the blood he bore within him. When he brought the house down he had already been applauded for a good five minutes by the two Myriams, by Bicou, by 'the old man', by the male and female Quasimodos and even, perhaps, by the 'forty franc father'. When the bladder-lovers carried him shoulder-high he was quite unconcerned for his glory, he slept like a satisfied lover.

So, on leaving prison, he had saddled his horse at a friend's who had looked after it for him and had returned to his delta. The country had changed a good deal; the region still lived tragically but was now used only as a setting. Even the sea. Even the gilded flotsam of the sea. He felt confusedly that a day would come when the great rectangle of Aigues-Mortes itself would be shattered like the seashells he heard smashing in the sand under his horse's feet.